666

First edition published by Spare Change Books, 1995.

ISBN: 978-1-60486-331-4
LCCN: 2011927955

Cover and interior design by Josh MacPhee/Justseeds.org.
Cover based on previous editions and Blinko's original cover illustration.

PM Press
PO Box 23912
Oakland, CA 94623
www.pmpress.org

Printed in the USA.

NICK BLINKO

THE PRIMAL SCREAMER

PM PRESS

INTRODUCTION

Roger Neighbour, MA, FRCGP

I recently heard the novelist Margaret Drabble and her husband the biographer Michael Holroyd discussing the rival claims of fiction and non-fiction as paths towards understanding. The debate was entertaining, but only in the sense that a firework display is entertaining. Then at question time someone in the audience stood up and wondered whether, in their search for truth, human beings are capable of anything **other** than fiction. Doesn't everything we express, no matter how "truthful" we intend it to be, come out distorted by virtue of having passed through our individual and unique minds?

People often say they want to know "the truth". But even more than truth, we crave meaning. Unless we can make our experiences "mean something"—and that's what our brains are for—we flounder and drown in a torrent of overwhelmingly arbitrary circumstances. Truth is just whatever, for now, gives events enough meaning for us to get by on.

So truth comes in different flavours, according to whatever experiences would be meaningless without it. Scientific truth, judicial truth, literary truth and mystical truth can all be different, yet equally valid.

Fifteen years ago, early in my career as a general practitioner, I thought I knew a lot of psychological truths. I'd had training in counselling and psychotherapy, Jungian analysis, Gestalt and family therapy. All can be good ways of imparting meaning to a wide range of human distress. But the distress of one young man, who slashed his wrists in a lonely thicket and could no more tell me why than could a newborn baby explain why it cries, would not be coaxed into any of these frameworks. It was powerful and violent; nonverbal. Preverbal. Then one day as I was trawling through his memory for clues, his voice trailed off. He drew his knees up to his chest, and his head inclined more and more to the left until his head was almost down onto his shoulder. Something infantile about his appearance made me ask, "How old do you feel right now?" The reply came at once: "No age at all".

In Zen there is a saying, **"When the pupil is ready, the Master appears"**. At that time, the end of the 1970s, humanistic psychiatrists such as Arthur Janov, R. D. Laing, Bill Emerson, Stan Grof and Frank Lake were developing concepts of birth trauma, intra-uterine memory, "the hostile womb". And what gave value to their ideas was that they led to what the hard language of science calls "therapeutic interventions"—ways of working with the victims of embryonic trauma that might, if not rewrite the prenatal record, at least spring the lock on the prison of its effects.

Well, I tried. And the rest is history.

History? Or fiction? As you read Nick Blinko's story, you may feel less sure than you did of the difference between fact and fantasy, between science and metaphor. Who better knows the landscape—the mapmaker or the traveller? At all events, I in my way and Nick in his both know the truth of George Santayana's epithet, **"Those who cannot remember the past are condemned to repeat it"**.

March 1995

1979

TUES NOV 20

This day has been the most harrowing of my career to date. A young man was ushered into the surgery by his mother. As the drastic nature of his condition became apparent, I was sent for immediately.

Both his wrists had been cut, as deep as is possible without actually severing the arteries, which were semiexposed and quivering. He hadn't lost much blood. That which had been spilt was nevertheless a frightening purple colour. Fortunately, thick clots had already formed on the wounds. He had only slight feeling at the base of his thumbs, but otherwise his hands functioned perfectly. I was hurriedly informed that the case was an attempted suicide. **He had really meant it.**

I was greatly shocked. My stomach turned. The young man apologised for being a burden and for the obvious distress he was causing me; common enough sentiments among such cases. He also stated that **this place** was not where he had intended to be, as if he had failed to reach some preordained destination. I believe he said these things partly in reaction to the nurse who, in her fright, was muttering under her breath the cliche "it's a cry for help" and generally tut-tutting. Rather than offering the insight of amateur psychology, her response was more an effort to calm herself. I must have a word with her about this.

It is never pleasant dealing with emergency cases, but at least one can normally label such incidents as genuine accidents and quickly tend to the injury. However, I have never—even during my training—seen such grievous self-inflicted injuries as those that lay upon the wrists of Nathaniel Snoxell.

Within the hour, using a new "freezing" spray aerosol as a makeshift local anaesthetic, I had completed the stitching of his horrific lacerations. I found the work went better if I imagined myself stringing my violin. The nurse completed treatment with lints and bandages and an overall clean up of the affected areas, whilst I spoke with the young man's mother. I had seen the knife he had used and an antitetanus injection wasn't necessary—not that they're of any real use, save as placebos. The youth and I then retired upstairs to my room, the remainder of my afternoon schedule being cancelled. Two greatly appreciated cups of tea were brought up to us.

I had never met Nathaniel before, his family doctor being one of my colleagues. The patient was tall and thin, slightly bent over, with short but wild black hair erupting over a high dome-like forehead. In fact, his head seemed too heavy for his neck to support and he held it to one side, virtually resting it on one shoulder. His eyes were very piercing yet somehow old. They were almost as black as his hair; an impression intensified by the glowing whiteness of his face. Dressed entirely in black he was on the darker, Gothic side of Romantic. He was not exactly clumsy in his movements, but he was self-conscious to a painful degree. He surveyed the view from my window whilst eagerly sipping his tea, which was piping hot. A somewhat fastidious appetite was, at least, intact, as he would take neither sugar nor milk. Eventually I coaxed him into a chair. I thought he looked like a mad doll, but quickly dispensed with the dangerous preconceptions suggested by his appearance, and began the gentle probing of his psyche.

"Well, what do I call you?" My usual opening gambit in such situations.

I already knew his strange and peculiarly pronounced name from the brief conversation I had had with his mother: "Nathaniel Snoxell".

"That's perfect iambic pentameter!" I had exclaimed.

"Yes", she had said, suddenly calm. "He was a very poetic baby".

I wondered, however, if he preferred to be called by an abbreviation or nickname. I had expected at best a morose reply, but was surprised by his smile and his laughter. So many things, it seemed, had to be contained within that laughter.

"Nat".

This high-pitched, monotone, monosyllabic form of verbal communication was, I soon found, greatly favoured by him and, at first, he practiced it almost exclusively. It had taken him a long time to reply, and after the utterance he returned to studying the pattern of my carpet.

"Well, Nat, where do we go from here?" I prodded. "Usually people are carted off to mental hospitals for what you've just done". I was attempting to provoke him into responding. "It's not exactly Britain's favourite way of ending it all, is it?"

Between long pauses he informed me of his high ideals and how the cruel world had shattered all his hopes; a familiar enough story. He grimaced frequently, lending pathos to each precisely worded statement. Nat had a magical reverence for certain things which had only recently been dashed. He had struggled to break free of his family, but the ties with his childhood had proved too strong, and he had allowed his mother to brow-beat him into finding work, in a toy shop. This was the antithesis of all his artistic and spiritual ideals. He had therefore decided to annihilate his existence.

So few and far between were his ejaculations that I had to be wary of putting words into his mouth and could not tell for sure if the picture I was building up of him was true, or merely a fabrication purposely designed to trap me.

Of the violence itself, he said the following. His parents had gone to work. His elder brother, who works the night-shift at a helicopter factory, was asleep. Funny, I'd had Nat down as an only child! His younger brother, with whom he shares a room, was at school. First Nat had tried jabbing at his arm with a variety of bizarre sharp objects. These included a jawbone of unknown origin, and some eighteenth-century scissors. (Perhaps a tetanus was in order after all.) Then he had taken a kitchen knife, which had recently been sharpened by his father, who was once a saw-doctor. Such personal minutiae seemed to obsess the gawky youth. This knife was the one the nurse and I had seen. Then Nat had set out for a nearby wood, "Oval Wood" I believe he called it. He had known it as a child. It was here that Nat had hacked away at his wrists but, he claimed, become too bored with the murderous task to finish the job. Lacking this passion, he had returned home, where his mother found him when she got back from her part-time work.

"It must have been very painful". I found myself adopting his pathos-filled grimaces. Although I quite often choose to mirror patients' expressions, this reaction was involuntary.

He spoke slowly but bravely of the most painful emotions, but refused to discuss sex. The abrupt ending of his spiritual quest had brought to the surface some previous conflict which he had been obliged to reenact.

We spoke, and gazed into space and at one another, for over two hours. His eye contact was good, if a little alarming at times. Eventually I concluded that he wasn't mad and informed him of my verdict. He looked a little disappointed, as if he felt he might belong in an "asylum", but it was difficult to tell. Whatever was happening to him was happening **internally**.

I told Nat I had some free time, late in the afternoons, and would be more than content to see him. I also informed him that I was well qualified psychologically speaking. We mutually agreed on an appointment for the following day. I gave him my card and he read it softly to himself: "Dr. Rodney H. Dweller M.A., M.B., B.Chir., D.Obst., R.C.O.G. . . ."

Afterwards I spoke again with his mother, and also his father, who by this time had been summoned from work. They seemed immensely grateful that I was taking the case on. Money was not mentioned. Instead I advised them not to allow Nat to let his hands flop, for he appeared to be all too ready to take on the guise of an elderly invalid.

The look in his eyes didn't belong to a youth of eighteen. I felt that the secret of what those eyes had gazed upon would not be surrendered lightly. It was this demoniacal-visionary aspect of Nat that has made my day so utterly disturbing, and not merely the physical carnage, upsetting though that was. However, I felt we had established a useful contact and, despite remaining darkly morbid and speaking openly of his desire for death, it was my belief that Nat would not suicide. My intuition detected within him a strand—a spark—of something strong. I felt that this would sustain him through the problematical days that inevitably lay ahead of us. I had made him promise to contact me if, at any time, he felt he would kill himself, and had sufficient confidence in him not to burden him with drugs, which would only compound his worries.

TUES NOV 27

Over the last week Nat has seen me each afternoon, at the surgery on week-days and at my home at the weekend. It is as regular as clockwork. Actually, he is the most punctual and polite young person I have ever worked with.

On Friday, whilst examining his wrists, some pus squirted in my eye. No infection has yet developed.

Nat's death wish is both incredibly deep-rooted and close to the surface. Ergo, most of the psychotherapy had centred around his strong desire for oblivion. Throughout the week I have been gleaning fragments of information regarding childhood traumas, and I can now assemble what is known more or less as a "normal" childhood, whatever normal means. There were the usual infant tears caused by falling down stairs, wetting the bed, fear of the dark etc. More revealing is what he chose to find relevant.

A spell in hospital, for what in its time was a routine childhood operation, was seen by Nat as a cosmic experience: "The sky made an evil yellow pattern". This, he claimed, was nothing to do with it being the first separation from his parents.

I have simply no experience whatsoever of what he describes as "doom-laden" feelings, nor the utter desolation and loneliness he senses lurking somewhere within him at all times. He speaks of being sucked upstairs, into the darkness, away from the rest of his family. This fantasy dates from the third year. Most striking of all his childhood images is the concept which he had been formulating, and brooding upon, up to the age of five. Namely, that he was the **only** human being and all others were aliens examining him.

The patient soon dispensed with usual and more obviously ego-related childish notions, such as the idea that one **is** Jesus Christ. In fact, he became revolted at the thought that he had once readily entertained so infantile a notion.

Also anno aetatis quintus suae Nat was constructing small books from scraps of paper. Few of these curious creations survive, but when they drove Nat to my house on Saturday, the family showed me one example, which described the macabre journey of a worm into a crow's belly and its eventual escape into outer space—cleverly illustrated to boot.

This was made at the time when Nat had played chess for the county: in the third team, on a low board, in a high chair. He had learnt the moves from watching his father playing a friend. "Pictures of moves" had entered his head. Although he had no idea of how to set up the pieces, somehow he could devise beautiful combinations, many moves deep. He still remembered some, despite having long since discarded the lovingly written scoresheets made at the time by his father. Nat had defeated skilled and experienced players, some many times his age. One of his more youthful victim-opponents has since recovered enough poise to go on and become European Hexagonal Chess Champion, whatever that is. However, Nat rapidly grew bored with chess and ceased to play altogether, claiming he had imagined every game of chess there could ever be. This was after he had defeated Vasily Smyslov, who had been World Champion a few years before. In a simultaneous display, Nat was the only one out of thirty players to obtain a result against the Soviet. Perhaps he was embarrassed by his success. He spoke of the futility of pushing pieces of wood about a board and mumbled about having fallen hopelessly under the spell of the Black Queen. His style of play had been similar to the American Grandmaster Bobby Fischer, whom he identified as the last in a long line of innovative geniuses of the game. Nat had particularly admired Fischer, who "ate, breathed and slept chess". After Fischer, said Nat, the theory and practice of chess would merely degenerate into a regurgitation of what had gone before. He had this same pessimistic view of most subjects, as if they'd reached their final states of development and awaited only apocalypse.

But not music. Music, he insisted, had scarcely been born. The world of harmonics and ultrasonics lay waiting to be tapped.

After this, Nat was sent to a nursery run by nuns. He came home screaming on the first day, begging his parents never to send him to "those

VASSILYSMYSLOV

Iambic
a
b
y

C.C.C.P.

slight lack of resemblance

world title contender

GRANDMASTER

black witches" again. All the other children in the neighbourhood had by this time started school, but as he was younger, he was allowed to stay at home with his mother and his younger baby brother. Nat wandered around the garden examining things in minute detail. Once he cut a red admiral butterfly into tiny little pieces: the logical conclusion of much time spent studying and modifying its wing structure. He also had a "pet" butterfly: it always came back to him, but only because he had rubbed the scales from its wings.

Then Nat became a vegan; a particularly severe form of vegetarianism. His father had taken him on one of his business calls, which happened to be to a man at an abattoir. The man, dressed in dingy white overalls, spattered with blood and worse, wielded a massive carving knife (could this be relevant?) whilst in conversation. The sight of this "butcherman" and the atrocities he saw there made Nat vow never to touch meat again. To me this seems an obvious, if understandable, denial of the hunting impulse. Thousands of years of instinct surely cannot be wiped out in a single generation.

Nat was so shocked that, for five years, he had been eating the corpses of animals and had even inflicted pain upon little creatures himself that he began to construct birds' nests and other homes for all manner of suburban wildlife. Some beasts even took to these ready-made "homes". Cats were particularly attracted to the infant and even spoke to him in their own language, not the usual "miaows" which he informed me were reserved with disdain for other humans.

With his younger brother Nat had concocted a secret language, a common enough thing for siblings to do, though this was quite a deep and rich lore involving a vast array of fantasy figures and high-pitched obscure utterances. The brothers shunned the television, unlike their older sibling who watched it incessantly. The only memory Nat cared to disclose in which both of his brothers featured involved a "ball of fire" which chased them all round the garden. He saw it as important that it followed them exactly; but it was only a stray piece of paper, from a bonfire, blown by the wind.

When Nat started school he adapted his behaviour to resemble that of his peers. Perhaps we all do this; not everyone is able to, but he certainly faded into the background. He remained outstanding at art, winning numerous competitions. Even then, however, he destroyed his crayoned efforts. A teacher had said that if the pupils didn't want their drawings, they should leave them at the school to be stored, or hung on the wall: on no account should they ever throw pictures away. Nat tore one of his drawings to shreds and dropped the remains in the churchyard which he walked through every day, to and from school. A fellow pupil, a little girl in the class above Nat's who lived only a few doors from his own house, discovered the misdemeanour and took a fragment to show the teacher. Nat complained that those **colours** could never be his. The little girl, however, had cleverly chosen the one piece of paper that bore his childish signature. This little incident did not change his attitude towards his pictures. He needed to make something, but not with the wise elders watching over his shoulder.

The friends he chose were invariably outsiders, who eventually came to reject him; or else their families, with an uncanny regularity, moved away from the area; or they became very ill. This bad luck with relationships also dogged his father, whose idea of helping Nat back to normality has been to recount in great detail his own entire life history.

"Ah, the curse of the Snoxells", I quipped, much to Nat's amusement. He tried to make something of the child repeating the parent's experience, but I could tell he despised such a notion.

By the time he was nine, Nat was an avid collector of fungi, placing the caps on paper and preserving the patterns made by the spores. Later he was found to be allergic to such fungal emissions and his huge collection of spores was destroyed. He did, however, go on picking a wide variety of toadstools and mushrooms to cultivate and to eat, but only after a course of injections had made him immune to the minute seedlings.

Nat was most careful to recount any scrap of information he felt might be helpful, within his own limitations: he still refused to discuss sex.

Nothing seemed of any use. Although the childish memories brought many smiles to his face he continually reiterated his intention to take his life.

"Well, it won't be the first death in a family", I found myself uttering in desperation.

FRI NOV 30

It is becoming clear that whatever troubles Nat to the very core of his existence will not be found within the conscious memories of childhood. It is important that he realises this.

I have several wild theories, the least improbable being that some buried trauma, sustained early in life, is now too harsh to exist anywhere other than deep in his subconscious. In order to try and discover if his conscious mind was guarding a dark secret, I resorted to some psychological games.

I asked Nat to write down all the thoughts that entered his mind in a fixed period of time. He brought me the results on a pitiful shred of paper, written in pencil. With the use of a magnifying glass I found the result was a stream of consciousness of which Joyce would have been proud. Although it was fascinating reading—1950s, plastic-face, sky-wall, mentalhead, coral-brain etc. etc.—none of it gave any real clue as to the source of his disturbance.

The next attempt was the completion of another list, this time of twenty sentences each beginning "I am". I also undertook to fill out my own potted biography, as it were. His list took in a vast cosmic sweep, scarcely revealing his self-image at all, it was so defensive. Again it seemed of no help. One sentence, however, still intrigues me: "I am hidden". I kept his list. He glanced over mine, which in stark contrast to his was very matter of fact: I am a G.P., a teacher, selfish, thirty-three, short, kind, a good cook, an amateur art historian, a psychologist, Zen Buddhist, single etc. etc. It showed off all my achievements, and I was a little hurt when he said he didn't want to keep it. "Renaissance man", he chortled.

The next game we played was sitting on the floor taking it in turns to look at one another for sixty seconds. Nat was clearly even more self-conscious than usual, and looked anywhere but at me for the whole minute. It was the longest time in all our meetings without him looking in any way at me.

SAT DEC 1

I've come to care a lot for Nat. I'm worried, as we don't seem to be getting anywhere and his death wish is as strong as ever. He has taken to not shaving or washing. His mother had informed me of this when I met her in the village last week; yes, I had already noticed. She spoke about herself being an only child. I told her that I was too, and through therapy had managed to overcome the feeling I'd had, that I was such a terrible disappointment to my parents that they'd chosen not to have any more children. Her childhood was much better balanced, and she had enjoyed the freedom known solely to the only child.

During one session, I gave Nat a mirror and asked him what he felt about the person he saw there. He smiled. His teeth have taken on a particularly worrying luminous shade of yellow. Despite their uncanny glow, there is, thankfully, no accompanying halitosis.

"Kill him", came the chilling reply.

"You callous bastard", I heard myself shout. Then a little more sympathetically, I asked him to tell me how he felt. "It doesn't matter if it sounds like a cheap nineteenth-century novel; it doesn't have to be earth-shattering. Come on, Nat! At this moment I'm able to run intellectual rings round you. Are you always like this?"

He stared at the sky and eventually said he felt sorry for me, for all I had to put up with.

"I can handle that myself, Nat", I replied. We laughed. Nat knows the suicide rate is highest amongst doctors, especially those who practice psychiatry or psychology. The analyst-patient relationship balances precariously; simultaneously both distanced and intimate. I believe that many of its faults lie with too rigid an adoption of the traditions laid down by the early pioneers.

I was glad to see that his physical wounds, at least, were healing. Nat was a little shocked at just how rapidly the dressings became lighter. Aware of his sensitivity to the passage of time, I asked him how old he felt.

"No age at all" he eventually uttered.

FRI DEC 21

It has now been one month since I first met Nat. I have declared him fit enough for light work, though I continue to sign for his sickness benefit to which, as his mother pointed out, he is entitled. I feel that Nat should be able to hold down a job, and that this would be very therapeutic, demonstrating his fitness.

Over these last four weeks Nat has shunned his friends, forcing his family to take phone calls. He never overcame a childhood aversion to telecommunications. He never answers the door. Inquisitive acquaintances are informed that "Nat is not at home at the moment". He tells me that his peers are not true friends, but just people "you're thrown together with at school".

He insists that he is not pessimistic about relationships, but seeing as how he's taken on such a reclusive lifestyle, significantly more sequestered to my mind than before his blow-up, it does not seem imminent that he will become involved. It certainly seems, at least from the outside, that Nat is still very fragile. **Delicate.**

Apart from his family and myself there has been just one other personage Nat has deigned to see. Simeon's family have known Nat's family for many years, and Nat and Simeon's friendship has grown over the last few years. Simeon is an artist: a B.A., at present taking a year out as a "ward skivvy"—nursing assistant at a psychiatric hospital. He shares many of Nat's obsessions, although not to the same degree. Nat says there is a kind of bond between them: an inability to get on with other people, I gather. Simeon has visited Nat several times since hearing of the suicide attempt. It seems he was thinking of doing something similar: patricide, I think. Nat was keen to impress upon me that Simeon's family live in a 1930s mock Tudor house, which Simeon had left when seventeen to go to art school. Simeon "probes" Nat in a very heavy-handed manner, a sort of pseudopsychology, from what I can discern. Apparently he took an A-level in sociology and failed it. I consider him a relatively harmless influence on my patient. His questioning is crude in the extreme. He bullies Nat relentlessly with hours of such aimless interrogation. Simeon suggested Nat should pay me a token sum from his sickness benefit, but Nat sarcastically pointed out that this custom originated because of Freud's religious background.

It is still proving very difficult to get to the root of Nat's illness. His depression follows the classic pattern of being harshest in the morning and lessening as the day wears on. It has slightly lessened its grip of late, but Nat is still at risk. In many respects Nat is very stubborn, but I cannot stay angry with him for more than two minutes at a time. I have never known such wayward charm. At times, though, he feels murderous. Paradoxically, I know he has the wherewithal to kill himself and yet I do not think that he could ever kill another person: he is emphatically one who could not deliberately injure a fly.

Encouragingly, he still does some household chores, the only male in the family to do so. He also still insists on cooking his own food.

At first, one or other of his parents stayed off work to be with him—in case. Each member of the family dragged him out to various places, in what proved to be futile attempts to show him what they found so positive about life. Even Simeon inundated him with his own brand of propaganda, if indeed Zen can be called propaganda. Each of these acts was undoubtedly undertaken with the greatest sincerity, but they have all served only to make Nat feel even more alienated than ever. He is essentially apathetic, lying in bed virtually all day, glancing at the blue sky or watching cloud formations.

Usually patients are reluctant and frequently relapse in psychoanalysis, but not often are they as secretive as Nat regarding sex. Whilst I greatly admire him for the way in which he speaks so openly of his most painful thoughts and feelings, and let him know so, I also tell him how childish I find his refusal to discuss sex.

Recently, more subtle approaches on the subject have run like this: "What are your fantasies?"

"I don't have any".

"Oh, I thought everyone has fantasies".

"No".

There was a brief silence. It struck me that he was obviously lying. "What have you been doing today?"

"Oh, thumbing through a book called *The Outsiders*".

"Are you an outsider?"

"No. These people had a special contact within; they shunned outside interest. Their special insights were born of their raw art, to which they dedicated much energy. Do not be deceived by the name given to these individuals".

"Don't you feel ashamed of what you did?"

"No".

"You should". For once he wasn't dressed entirely in black. "Ah, not in mourning today, Nat". He did not begrudge me a laugh. In fact he still smiles a lot. **In between death wishes.** A most curious state of affairs, in fact. It is sad that he is not seeing any children. Such a smile would charm them and he would enjoy their company too.

At school Nat had been known as "zombie", presumably because of his "ancient" piercing eyes and skeletal face, and certainly not for his personality, which is essentially the opposite of his appearance. Once he tried to destroy all of his emotions, so as to become a purely intellectual being. Needless to say the harder he tried, the more poignant was his failure in this bizarre quest.

Things he talks freely of, but which hold little interest for me, are dreams. Nightmares: a "deathman" stalks him, garbed in even blacker apparel than Nat himself. I said that some people think dreams important and some people think them unimportant. He was somewhat taken aback that anyone could find dreams unimportant. He clearly has a high regard for them—a reverence—ergo I heard him out. I did not contradict his earlier denial of fantasies.

Nat feels okay about the Christmas period. It will be a quiet one for his family this year. I made a time to see him. I said I hate this time of year, having to carry two appointment diaries about all the time.

I wonder if hypnosis would be effective on Nat. I have given very successful hypnotic treatments to patients for minor ailments, in general practice. Those to whom I have given hypnosis for more serious complaints have also responded well. From my data, I would judge Nat a bad subject. It is, however, notoriously difficult to predict just who will have a resistance and who will be compliant.

THU DEC 27

I explained to Nat that his psychoanalysis cannot go any further unless we unearth whatever it is that troubles him enough for him to desire to take his own life. He agreed to try the hypnotism, probably out of the sheer boredom into which his life has degenerated. I wasted no time. I began the routine of asking the patient to tighten, then release one by one, toe to head, every muscle in the body. This should occur at a slow pace, in conjunction with deep breaths, tensing and exhaling whilst releasing the muscles, in order to achieve maximum relaxation. (Apparently Nat had never relaxed in his life!) The patient then raises one arm at full length, just above the head with thumb outstretched, the path of which is then followed by the eyes as it gradually falls, to the somnambulistic coaxing of my voice. When the eyes are shut, the patient pictures himself descending ten steps, which I count down until the full hypnotic trance is reached.

This phase went well enough with Nat. He stayed in the trance for two hours experiencing the usual heightened awareness, well-being, rapid but pleasant passage of time, and memory of being in similar though less deep states. He is happy enough to continue tomorrow and is surviving the festive season reasonably well.

FRI DEC 28

This time I showed Nat the power of hypnosis. I always feel more like a witch-doctor than usual at such times. The hypnotic trance being rapidly obtained, I placed a sterilised needle under the skin atop his right hand, with no pain induced. Nat seemed duly impressed and eager to use the new-found force to reveal the source of his misery. His ideas were running wild on the subject: from having been molested as a child, unfortunately more common than he thinks, to maybe even committing and then forgetting a murder, happily not so ubiquitous as he imagines. His fantasies were all quite normal: the vast majority of the concepts lie safely within the bounds of flight of thought and at quite a far remove from the frenzied excesses of schizophrenia.

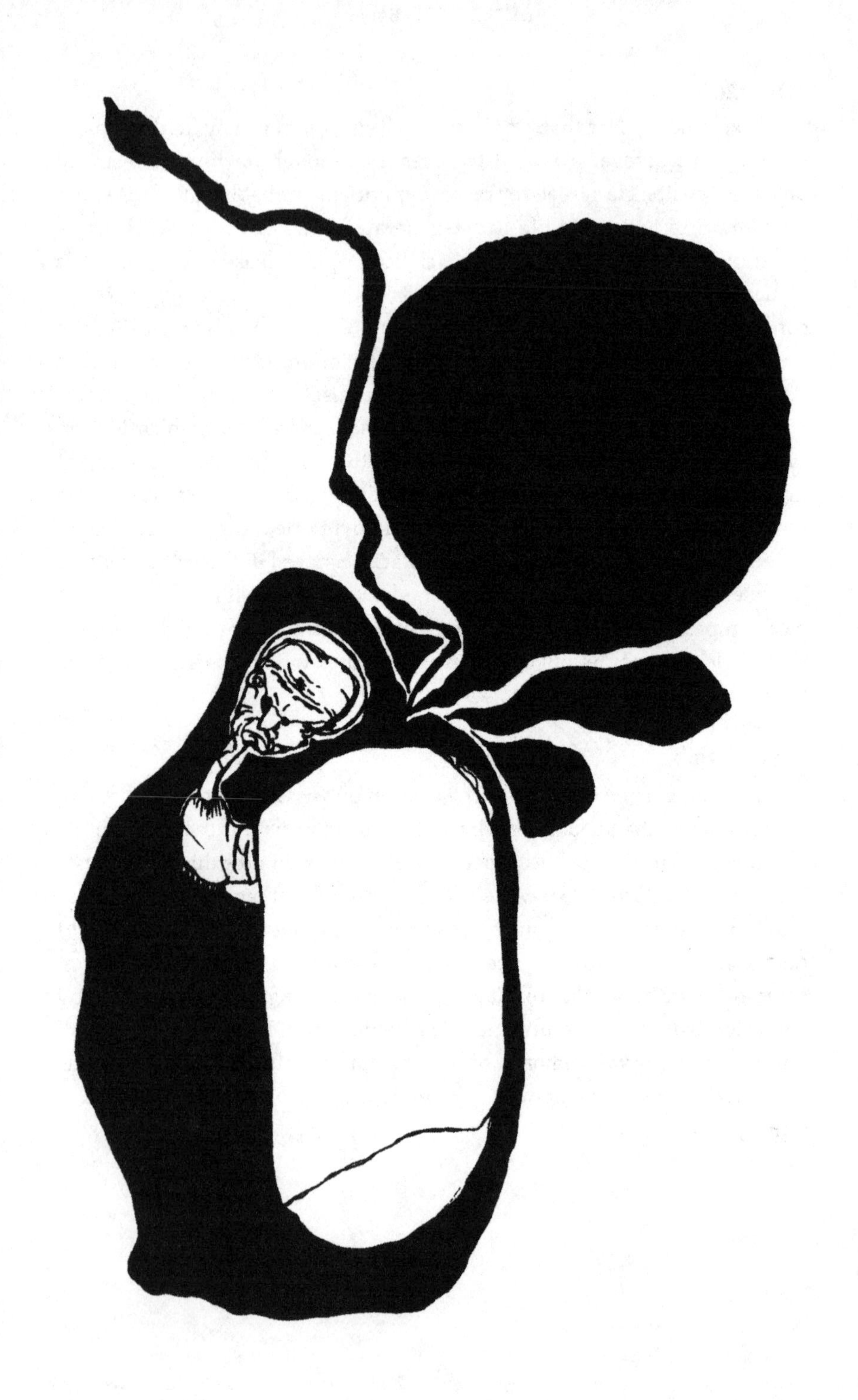

1980

figure 3.
"a hoopoe bird"

from Nat's nature notes of 1972

figure 23.

"Belgic Pottery"

as drawn by Mr. Thistle

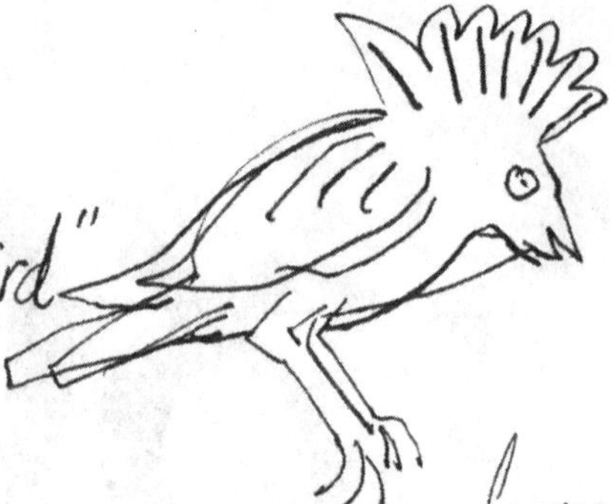

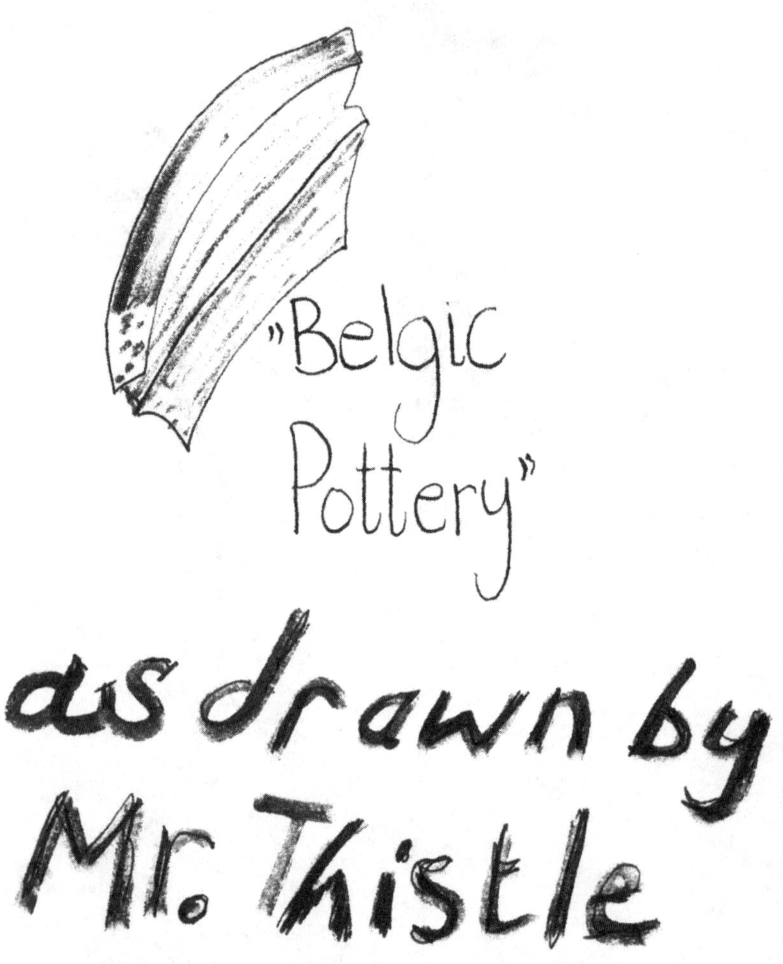

THU JAN 3

On the third day of hypnosis I took Nat back to his childhood. All quite in order; butterflies and sunrays particularly prominent. A beautiful memory was retrieved: once, he stuck out his tongue and saw tiny, brightly coloured people dancing in a circle upon it. Fear of school, sibling rivalry. All natural events.

After this, Nat began cutting out. He refused to let go. He was not, however, anal-retentive. His mother, who gladly parted with this information, had wisely allowed her children to learn bowel control at a natural rate, and they had matured faster and more happily because of this. He spent more and more time in the hypnotism sessions veering towards the fully conscious state. I let him know in no uncertain terms how infuriating I found this. It seems pointless to continue.

SUN JAN 6

At least Nat's personal hygiene has improved, but his hair is growing disturbingly fast. I am at a dead end with him. I have spoken with his parents and they have agreed to come to a meeting, to talk with Nat and myself. This ought to embarrass him into some kind of confession. I've gone from feeling like a witch-doctor last week to feeling like a witch-hunter this week.

THU JAN 10

Today I had my first session with Nat and his parents.

I thanked them for the big box of biscuits which they had sent me over the festive season. They must have found out my favourites from the surgery receptionist. They went over Nat's entire life: how he was as a child—the family favourite—to loss of interest in school and the present development of nocturnal habits. Virtually everything they mentioned was known to me.

Nat squirmed in his chair: it was "like having the family album of photographs shown to your worst enemy" he later hissed in a dry aside.

Nat's parents cannot understand why their son does not simply "pull himself together". They are sick of seeing him in pyjamas, dressing-gown and slippers, slouching around the house during the day and getting up to mysterious practices at night.

They complained that Nat refuses to let them kiss or hug him.

"What eighteen-year-old does not reject paternal affection?" I asked. They took the point, but not whole-heartedly, unable to see this as a healthy attribute.

They were pleased he still smiles often. Yes, I agreed, but also admitted to not quite having worked out the reason for the smile. Both parents are intelligent but have settled for jobs below their capabilities. They are somewhat disillusioned, even though they share a lively sense of humour. Despite all the quirks or because of them, I think they function extremely well together. Quite singular family dynamics.

Nat's parents were intrigued by the hypnotism he had undergone. His mother felt it must be okay and recalls people surviving "going under" in the 1930s, prior to having a tooth pulled. I agreed with her on the strength of hypnosis and informed her that its noble history stretches back many thousands of years further than its dental application in the early twentieth century.

The session shed light on some facets of Nat's life which I had previously overlooked. It had not sunk in just how **weird** his existence has become. In retrospect, his hair has seemed longer by the day. I vaguely recollect him expounding a theory that we should all allow our hair to grow as long as possible, so as to render clothing and shelter redundant, and preserve resources: a "hair home" he called it. Very strange. Being still unable to fully verbalise the torment within him, his body is doing it for him instead. **Eloquently.**

I pondered for a long time on the many curious and fascinating contortions Nat can perform during the course of a conversation. I have developed a system whereby I can discern his mood simply by the angle and incline of his head and neck. The way his fingers can bend backwards, as though aroused or perchance divining for something, is almost oriental, and most off-putting. His peculiar performance reminds me of something, but what? I just cannot tell. It is a type of double-jointedness I have not encountered before.

MON JAN 14

Nat has confided in me that he has weeping fits quite often, but only when alone. Occasions when he has actually broken down and cried until, as they say, one can cry no longer, have been very rare. This coincides exactly with a description of a certain visionary people's characteristics in a homeopathic book I've been reading. I shall not, however, follow the suggested cure. Homeopathy **is** good, but only for minor ailments.

THU JAN 17

Nat seemed more distant today than of late. The atmosphere in my room oppresses him. I should dearly love to dispose of my desk but fear such a move would outrage more patients than it would please.

Nat keeps talking about suicide. I called his bluff: what method would he try this time? No, I didn't advise jumping, screaming from the top of a tall building. Why? Because I know a man who has to clear up the mess.

"Oh", said Nat, "but we don't want him to swell the ranks of the unemployed, do we?"

He talked of pills. In desperation I asked him to let me know when he feels suicidal. He nodded but, I fear, only to keep me quiet. So I spelt it out to him, saying that I didn't want to be left with a corpse on my hands. I pointed out that either he goes back and makes a better job of it, or we get down to some serious work **now**. This seemed to stir him. I attempted once more to coax him into talking about sex. Why wouldn't he talk about sex? English stiff upper lip? If it was performance, homosexuality, bisexuality etc. I said I could relate to such problems. He said it was none of these, but assured me that if he felt close to taking his life he would be in touch.

There seems to be no way he can release his immense and genuine anger, save for when, on two recent occasions, I caught him looking at me with evil intent. I advised him to shout as loud as possible, in a secluded place, so as not to scare any innocent bystanders.

MON JAN 21

Nat has been screaming to some effect, but it is only a temporary respite. What did he shout? A secret word. He would not tell me.

WED JAN 23

Today was my second session with Nat and his parents. I call it "family therapy". Nat calls it a "postmortem". It proved to be a far more agreeable affair than expected. Nat appeared clean-shaven and neat, for him, although his hair is still long. A diagonal fringe, rather like that of Hitler (another non-carnivorous person), almost covers his left eye. His parents tried to cajole him into acknowledging that he possesses emotions other than blackest despair. Apparently they were overjoyed to see his pleasure in playing with a toy balloon. Another plaything—of Nat's own making—is less pleasing, being constructed chiefly from his discarded, festering, pus-soaked bandages.

Again his parents reeled out a string of quaint and charming happenings from Nat's childhood. It is hard to believe that this macabre youth was once such a charming child, unless, of course, one happens to be a strict Jungian. Nat's mother and father are still at the "where did we go wrong" stage. More helpfully, however, they lay the blame for their son's present condition upon various subcultures and occults which have preoccupied Nat's mind since early adolescence. He merely laughs at this. It is a menacing laugh; the parents' turn to become embarrassed. This is not a "paranoid" family as such, but it may well subconsciously have off-loaded its collective neuroses onto Nat.

FRI JAN 25

Today I visited Nat's home, just a short walk from my surgery. This house is the oldest—and one of the smallest—in the ancient village of Black Langley, birthplace of the only English Pope. This oddly named "Black Pope" was born at a site not far from Nat's house. It was at home in this strange structure that Nat had been brought into the world by one of my practice's more senior colleagues. He has lived there all his life, seldom venturing from the county, and certainly never setting foot outside these Isles. The history of his home is shrouded in mystery. His family inherited it, through puzzling twists of lineage, over thirty years ago.

Nat's room overlooks the village churchyard with its abundance of yew trees and two fine examples of the American redwood, wellingtonia. The bay window is so heavily latticed that the view is almost obscured. From the ivied encasement the garden itself looks almost unchanged since just after the ice age left it, save for the peculiar herb and fungal gardens of Nat's childhood design. One mushroom looked impossibly **green**, although I noticed no psilocybe or marijuana plants.

Nat had invited me down in the early evening to look over some drawings he'd been working on. His half of the room was covered in black paint onto which he had etched and scratched eldritch sketchwork, revealing the gaudy wallpaper beneath.

Nat's younger brother, with whom he shares the room, is an interesting case himself. He is referred to by all the family as "the child", despite being sixteen. He is a fine musician and spends much time improvising on a toy harpsichord which looks and sounds rather dubious. Composition is his forte. I suggested that he may well one day become a famous film composer. He plans to attend the Royal College of Music after securing the necessary A-level results; he already has good enough music grades. I always think people who go to the College are so much nicer than those who attend the Academy.

"The child" invariably has a kaleidoscope or a telescope pressed to one eye, in search of lunar rainbows and shooting stars in particular. Red striped confectionery of the American candy type dangles from his lips. Most inexplicably, he sports an old-fashioned little pink hearing-aid, of which I can find no mention in his medical records. Although the appearance that the "child" affects is to say the least eccentric, he nonetheless interacts well with his peers and teachers. And I believe that his reasoning was true when he said there were still some things he wanted to do before he grew up. It is nice to see childhood taking its own course and not suffering artificial termination at the age of nine or ten. "The child" knows how to have fun. I also gained the impression that the transition from childhood to adulthood would be quite easy and natural for him, unlike Nat who had preferred suicide to growing up.

The "child" has covered his territory with reams of manuscript paper, should inspiration seize him during the night. A bookshelf contained his Ladybird books and Nat's books about weird art and literature and the bizarre, sad life stories of its creators.

After leaving school, Nat had turned down a place at art college, in order to take the brave path of studying alone. He was slightly grudgingly supported by his parents, who hoped he would one day take up the opportunities a student life offers. The results of his endeavours had not pleased him, and few of his art pieces survived the onslaught of his ruthless perfectionism. A few canvases not destroyed occupy a corner, each carefully wrapped in several layers of tightly bound brown paper. Atop this sorrowful pile is a dusty pestle and mortar once used for mixing his own pigments. He had only used the most ancient solutions and concoctions. How he obtained knowledge of these techniques is a mystery: no art school teaches such formulae.

Nat's dressing gown, so despised by his father, hung from a hook on the door. It was still warm, for Nat had only recently dressed in anticipation of my arrival. He pulled out a tattered old portfolio and showed me the pen and ink drawings he'd been "dabbling with" since the violent onset of his illness. I had hoped to be positive about them, endorsing their therapeutic value, as it were. Nat, however, witnessed my horror at the sheer ghoulishness of his work.

"I like them", I said, "if indeed one can **like** such things. They're skilled, anyway. But what do you hope to obtain other than fluency with a pen?"

There was no reply. His drawing is undoubtedly ingenious, displaying considerable virtuosity and ability. It's the most intricate work I have ever seen, the detail incredible. But the subjects. . . This was where his anger had been going.

He understood what he was doing perfectly well. The evil that lurks within a Dore, or within folk tales of wonder and mystery, had been brought to the surface here wrought with great precision, and yet had not yielded any of its secrets or sacrificed atmosphere one iota. This was not the typical art of neurotics, nor could it ever find favour in the rarefied, hot-house world of galleries. Even within the narrow confines of horror movies, these illustrations would be seen as particularly macabre.

Their subject matter consisted entirely of grossly distorted ecorche heads. Nat said that these characters had perfected certain areas of their minds, overusing these faculties down the generations, resulting in the hideous enlargements. He had deeply contemplated such creatures' existences, elaborating phantasmagoric biographies for his creations. This came through in the drawings themselves: a kind of sympathy that does not show itself in Leonardo's grotesques, gothic gargoyles, nor indeed any other depiction of monsters I can think of. It was as if Nat **was** one of the things he portrayed, so vivid and intense was his vision. This is more than an outpouring of the subconscious such as in Francis Bacon. It does more than simply assail the nervous system. The only place for such art is obscurity. Perhaps there are other artists like Nat, their work being kept underground, or burnt when discovered. His art is most disturbing, and yet in spite, or because of its deathliness, it makes one feel incredibly **alive**.

"Are you happy with them?" I asked. "You should be". He did look a little proud. I informed him that many composers, artists etc. etc. had gone on to create much greater works after surviving life-threatening illnesses. He appeared more than a little pleased, as if in some small way his name had been added to a perverse roll-call of honour.

Executed in black and white as Nat's art is, I swear I could see **colours** in it. Weird colours. The strange house and mad garden must have affected my judgement. That garden! Who has ever heard of green fungus anyway? The spores must have been affecting me. I must get myself an allergy test.

When the family had all gone out Nat, showed me the cellar. A stone door was hidden beneath the stairwell-cupboard. More stairs led into the cellar itself. I am of no immense stature and yet had difficulty negotiating these steps. It was as if they' d been built by dwarves. However, Nat glided down with a grace about him I've never seen before. Incredibly, no one else knows of this extra room's existence. It was covered with a thick carpet of moss, lichen and sphagnum. Nat had some "pet"—he objected strongly to my use of the word—amphibians and silverfish here, and I took great care in not crushing any of these creatures beneath my feet. This was difficult as the room was so very confined; a veritable wood-cellar.

In one corner was a black box shedding sickly, bluish light. Gradually I perceived it to be an old television set. Nat explained that it had not been switched off for thirty years. Even so, I could see no cable emanating from the contraption. I had lost all sense of reality and so found this not hard to believe. An array of looking-glasses, contact lenses, maritime compasses and an astrolabe were strewn about the old television. Nat doesn't watch T.V. as normal people do, but meditatively and dreamily studies the cathode rays, or whatever those repulsive bluish hues are that so antique a television set emits.

Opposite the television was a full-length mirror. This was very strange too, although I still cannot define precisely why. By now I had noticed an abundance of potent smells, each separate and distinct in its own right, but occupying only a few cubic inches. The odours were not all bad; some even reminded me of intimates.

In the third corner lay a smashed shrine to some pagan or Greek deity: Pan, judging by the size of its severed penis, or perhaps it was a medical model designed to illustrate priapism—the only sexual reference I can recall in connection with Nat. The broken icon was compacted with dust, presumably having fulfilled its function some years ago, before its subsequent demise. These aberrations (or revelations) prompted many questions, but Nat led me to the fourth corner, the entrance to the enclave. Again he floated up the steps like an apparition, whilst I stumbled after him.

He led me away to the attic, clambering through a dismal hatch and throwing down a rickety ladder for me to struggle up after him. Nat's parents had told me of his nocturnal ramblings in this uppermost chamber. For—unlike the cellar—they knew about his love for this particular place.

He lit several candles. He seemed more active than I had ever seen him before. The ancient beams played off one another at the most curious angles, apparently not at all conducive to sound roof construction, although their age and proven architectural durability argued otherwise.

Nat beckoned me from another hiding place of his, a stubby gable with miniature black brickwork. From a variety of nasty dark hooks hung several skeletons, of human children, I imagined. I was casually informed that they had been excavated during the various alterations that the little house had undergone in the eighteenth century. They had not been reburied, for at the time the local graveyard had fallen prey to subterranean rivers. It was felt that the old bones, for even then they were very aged, should not come to rest outside of the parish. They had therefore been sealed in the attic and forgotten. Also dangling from a hook, swinging menacingly in a gentle aught, was the jaw-bone with which Nat had sought to take his own life. Bizarrely, it looked as if it had been sterilised.

Strewn about this cramped compartment were several other bones, some so decayed as to be mere piles of dust. In a corner, part obscured by shadow, lay something that resembled an Egyptian mummified baby, though by now I felt that I could not be shocked by anything that Nat might have in store for me. He was most gleeful at the way he had turned the tables on me; effectively reversing, at least temporarily, our relationship. He was the possessor of knowledge, albeit totally quack and charlatan, and I was the bewildered wretch in need of enlightenment.

I made an appointment to see Nat a few days hence. I was greatly relieved to escape the mad charnel house. I cancelled all evening engagements and spent the rest of the day practicing my violin for this month's chamber ensemble concert, in an effort to relax. That place should be declared unfit for human habitation, or hermetically sealed and opened as a black museum.

I realise I have totally failed to take into account the effect of environment in the case of Nathaniel Snoxell. The eldritch house, in which he lives, would fully explain his doom-laden feelings. Indeed, this aspect of his character is so firmly entrenched that he would cease to be 'Nat' without it. His younger brother is only superficially influenced by the morbidity of the house. Their elder brother is entirely untroubled by it, being obsessed by things mechanical and sexual. Indeed, he is so utterly different to the other two that when I mentioned this to his mother, she became agitated as if I was questioning the young man's parentage.

SAT JAN 26

It seems as if Nat's delicate nature and visionary aspect have made him the ideal foil for picking up so exclusively the grisly idiosyncrasies of the house. The rest of the family seems to exist firmly within the twentieth-century world which cloaks the ancient building, whilst Nat is a prisoner of a much earlier time, at least in his own mind.

The extent to which Nat is steeped in the macabre has greatly shocked me. Going on what his parents had told me, I had expected perhaps a few tawdry tokens: books, posters etc. from the rapidly expanding horror genre market. At worst I had expected tarot cards and ouija boards—which can actually unleash dormant psychical forces.

I was suspicious of the effects Nat's fungi garden might have had on my perceptions whilst visiting him. I therefore ran some tests and found that I have developed a mild allergy to fungal spores, but only certain rare varieties, of which Nat must have some examples. I've been studying some books on fungi; it would seem that some species are colonised by lichens and mildew—hence the green toadstool illusion. I believe it was the allergy that so distorted my sense of smell in the secret cellar. However, there is no accounting for that incredible television set, which supposedly has been running uninterrupted, barring power cuts, for thirty years; it is a possibility. Nor is there any accounting for the funny mirror, or the things which I beheld in that archaic attic.

SUN JAN 27

To find out more with regard to Nat's house, I contacted a local retired archaeologist, Mr. Thistle, who has a deep interest in the history of Black Langley, firmly believing that it has its origins in a Belgian iron-age settlement. I hinted at some of the things I had seen in Nat's house. He was not in the least perturbed, probably due to a lifetime's study of corpses and old graves, and living amongst ancient burial mounds during digs. Indeed, he informed me that many houses are built upon "boneyards", Black Langley being no less eager than other villages during the fifteenth century in its pursuit and destruction of heretics and witches. He considered that all houses were built on the resting place of some unfortunate, when you contemplate the number of deaths over the last ten thousand years.

These comments were not entirely jocular, nor were they far from the truth.

Mr. Thistle is a charming gentleman, over ninety years old, and very much a figure of the last century. He wears plus fours and hiking boots, frequently undertaking long meandering walks. He knows Nat's parents fairly well, and on several occasions went with Nat to Oval Wood. This was after Nat had found a piece of pottery there. His parents had laughed, but Nat had insisted that it be shown to the old archaeologist. Mr. Thistle had sent the shard to the British Museum for analysis, who returned it with the description: "carbon-dating revealed definitely pre-Roman, almost certainly Belgic pottery". Mr. Thistle had been delighted as this supported his Belgic settlement theory. It was after this that he and Nat went off together on many little expeditions to the wood, but never unearthed anything exciting. They did once see a rare and beautiful hoopoe bird—Nat mistook it for a giant butterfly, it was so colourful—but Mr. Thistle, a keen ornithologist, had recognised it instantly. He had not seen Nat since then, some ten years ago. Nat had become obsessed with dinosaurs, whereas Mr. Thistle's studies favoured the anthropological, and so they had drifted apart. How sad.

I wasn't shocked to hear of Nat's childhood adventures in the wood. He had already suggested as much, but I was rather surprised to learn that he had enjoyed the company of this Victorian gentleman. Previously I had built up a picture of his infancy as either being a private fantasy world shared with his younger brother, or else solitary.

Mr. Thistle regaled me with stories of curios and buildings in the area, particularly the vicarage, which he claims was once haunted: "seven times the north-east facing chimney was destroyed and seven times it was rebuilt. This was all in the last one hundred and seventy years. Only on the seventh occasion was there a vicar wise enough to exorcise the place and silence the ghost".

He spoke with the whimsy of one who had spent much time in sepulchres and grown immune to supernatural mysteries. Quite clearly, however, he believed what he was saying. "It's been quiet these last thirty years" he observed. "There's also a secret passage between the church and vicarage, which I helped to explore. I advised that it be sealed so as not to be a trap for inquisitive children".

Today was the first time that I had met Mr. Thistle, his doctor being one of my more senior colleagues. He is one of the last genuine **characters** left in Black Langley. It is peculiar, the way in which people, facts etc. drift into one's world. Although I have lived in and around Black Langley all my life, I find that I have never desired to know much about it. Perhaps I shall study the booklet which Mr. Thistle gave me. He had privately published this over a decade ago; the first fruit of his late retirement.

Mr. Thistle has a blind spot where Nat's house is concerned. He describes it in his pamphlet with a single word: "monstrosity". He is not the only one impervious to its charms. I have also discovered that despite its great age, it is not a listed building of any grade whatsoever.

It is one thing for a house to be accidentally built upon a graveyard, but quite another to actually preserve and maintain human remains in the attic. I am not as scared as I was after seeing Nat's horrible collection. His grim artistic "dabblings" are not **so** disturbing, after all. I believe this because, in retrospect, it was the first time he had shown genuine interest in anything since I learned of his depression, with its alarming presenting problem, eight weeks ago. "Unwholesome" as his obsessions are, they represent at least a step up from the relentless and singular death wish.

I still haven't discovered the root of Nat's depression. I feel that his morbid fascination is only a result of living in **that house**, but his disturbance goes much deeper. It occurs to me that I've been rather like a mother to him: he comes to me almost every day, and I fulfil many of his needs, both real and symbolic. The phrase that he wrote—"I am hidden"—still intrigues me. His behaviour is in many ways that of a baby. I have therefore decided to undertake a course of primal therapy with him. I have used this with a couple of cases over the last few years and it has been most beneficial. I too found it helpful when I undertook a special course during my training as a psychotherapist. I am a little apprehensive in that I've never practiced it on someone who is in such a deep state of despair. The only studies of such cases are American (more precisely Californian), where such therapies supersede one another at an alarming rate.

TUES JAN 29

I saw Nat today, our first meeting since he showed me his artworks and assorted bizarre objects. He spoke in great detail of another nightmare, which he called a dream, about a "Deathman" pursuing him in a crumbling sewer. It is easy to suggest that such nightmares are the product of a mind that has dwelt too long on fiendish things. I believe, however, that it is clinical depression that has led him down this path.

Nat confirmed my suspicion that the pattern of his life has more or less returned to its original state, except of course for the overt death wish. The doom-laden feelings have always been with him. He agreed that they are so great a part of his personality that he would feel lost without them. I put to him my analogy of the helpless baby, and a flash of recognition lit up his "old" eyes. Almost eagerly, he agreed to the proposed primal therapy. Had he not once said that he felt "no age at all"? We both concurred that this line of enquiry looked promising. I favour it because it relates much more to bodily memory, ergo it cuts through virtually all of the inhibitions that the patient may harbour in hypnotism, which relies on a conscious effort and a will to "let go".

I urged him to divulge the secrets of his two hidden chambers of horrors to his parents, but this he is loath to do. Why then had he shown them to me? I pointed out that it would be ethically correct for me to warn the family of the unknown dangers, seeing as how the old bones and antique television, if indeed it is a television, warrant health and fire risks respectively. He called my bluff on this, and he is right. I should not like to betray his confidence at this stage in the proceedings. The patient's recovery is ninety per cent his own making but the analyst must provide—solidly—the other ten per cent. After all, the Snoxells have survived well enough in their house up to now. In exhibiting to me his "skeletons in the cupboard" and his ghoulish gimcracks, he has made himself more anxious than me. His torpor is not that of a procrastinator, but serves instead to mask a multitude of seething emotions. The death wish and doom-laden feelings are only treatable in the short term with drugs, which I feel would be a cop-out. I have chosen to focus my attentions on the anxiety, for which the prognosis is good as I have had great success in helping people to relax more and be at ease in their relationship with life. It is frustratingly complicated to precisely define Nat's overall **mood**, although I can tell how he is when I am with him.

On days when he feels "better" and I ask him where all his death thoughts have gone, he is understandably reluctant to apply himself to such a disturbing question, whereas on other days the outlook for him seems unalterably bleak.

FRI FEB 1

I have just conducted the first primal therapy session with Nat, at my house. I didn't take it too far, as it was his initiation into a world we shall be extensively exploring together. First came the relaxation process which, as he noted, was the same as in hypnosis. I encouraged him to use this technique whenever he feels troubled, but I can't fully treat his anxiety unless he is willing. Next I placed my hand on his stomach. I was quite shocked at just how rapidly he assumed the foetal position. He was alarmed too at the new state of being into which he found himself so suddenly hurled. I maintained a calm verbal contact and brought him out of the experience within the hour.

Afterwards we discussed what had happened. He seemed very excited and described quite eloquently the phenomenon of dual consciousness. I explained that whilst he didn't remember being in his mother's womb as such, his body had perfect recall and could therefore trigger recollections in his mind. In essence, he was for the duration of the session both a foetus and an eighteen-year-old, with equal access to both spheres. He greatly relished this concept; clearly it was the most enlivening experience he'd had for some time. When I was fully satisfied that he had understood what had happened, and that he was firmly restored to his eighteen-year-old world, I took Nat back to his home. I explained to his mother what we had been doing. She couldn't conceive of all it had entailed, perhaps due to embarrassment over so revealing a form of curative treatment; one that also by its very nature necessarily involved her.

I agreed to explain the process more thoroughly: "Got your diary, Mrs. Snoxell?" We made a time.

SAT FEB 2

I saw Nat this afternoon, in order to ensure that he was not suffering any adverse effects from yesterday's delvings into his past. On the contrary he seemed positively invigorated by what he had been through. I was especially glad to see him, as there have been some incidents of suicide recently, in the States, by patients who had undergone primal therapy. Equally the beneficial attributes have been quite dramatic, and those that had taken their lives would most likely have done so regardless of their treatment. However, I must be more careful with Nat, as this would appear to be the first case in this country directly involving the connection between early development/ birth and overt death wish/suicide. I believe the field of primal therapy to be a most promising one; any erroneous publicity from the gutter press linking it with self-destruction could set back its cause five years or more.

Nat and I discussed bodily memory. He was most amazed that such a thing could exist, previously having taken for granted, as most people do, the body to be lacking in intelligence, merely responding to the brain's commands. I revealed to him my ability to assess his moods—when I'm with him—by the incline of his head and neck. This triggered in him a rambling speech about how people are conditioned via their bodily memories to be prisoners of the past, unaware and perhaps unable to alter their feelings and reactions. He expatiated to such a degree using this new-found "knowledge" that, for once, I actively had to shut him up.

MON FEB 4

Today I fell into conflict with Nat and his parents. They are most disgruntled that his behaviour has not changed. They are, however, happy for the primal therapy to progress. They seem a little relieved that my line of enquiry had taken me so far back. It is impossible for them to stop blaming themselves and their child-rearing for Nat's condition. They obviously seek exoneration through the success of this therapy.

Nat's mother soon returned to looking perturbed as I questioned her about the pregnancy of her middle son. Nothing untoward had occurred; it was a "normal" pregnancy. I did not press the matter as she was evidently most embarrassed by discussing the delicate topic. Nat had already described to his parents, in quite minute detail, just what exactly primal therapy entails. I therefore had to answer only a few remaining queries put to me by the family.

FRI FEB 8

Nat has returned to a prevailing mood of darkness following his mild elation in the wake of the first regression session. He even muttered some garbled nonsense about jumping into the path of an underground train. I said, callously, "don't do that Nat it's not very nice for the driver". I told him about a driver I know who has had precisely this ghastly experience. Surprisingly enough, this perverse conversation elicited a sympathetic response. I recalled his high regard for other living things, and saw in it an exteriorisation of the will to live, which in most people counter balances any desire for death. Early in childhood, Nat sought to protect life, for instance through his veganism. It is not totally illogical, I extemporised, that this expansion of life-enhancing energy into the world must also provide an equal compensation: that is, growth of the desire for death in the individual concerned.

Death is not something I care to discuss with Nat, for if I am willing to play the devil's advocate, I find Nat is invariably only too "happy" to play the devil. Nevertheless, I thought it would be useful to construct an accurate picture of his idea of death.

Does he know anyone who has died? No, two of his grandparents died before he was born, and the other two are still alive.

Has he ever seen a corpse? No, only the skeletons he keeps in that strange stubby gable, and what he has seen in museums. Oh yes, and as he passes the butcher's shop. It must be sad to see what the majority regard as food, as **corpses**.

What did he think happened to one after physical death of the body? A long silence. The only clue as to his thoughts was his erubescent face, for he blushes quite often. "How do you feel now?" I asked.

"Terrible", came the reply. Once negative thoughts and emotions assail him he seems hopelessly lost in a downward spiral of depression. Eventually he asked for **my** concept of death. I reeled off some Zen spiel but, in truth, my cultural, contractual, genetic and emotional inheritance conditioned me to feel little different to him in this respect.

WED FEB 13

The second primal therapy session with Nat. He arrived at my house at 8 p.m. sharp. After the initial relaxation stages he again went straight into the foetal position. Simulating wombic conditions, I umbilically prodded his belly button. He writhed around on the floor whilst I continued to worry at his stomach. Then came the screaming: unlike any noise I have ever heard. I was forcibly reminded of Isis who uttered cries that killed. What that poor boy has repressed for these last twenty years is inconceivable. Sangfroid deserted him completely and he kept losing control, succumbing entirely to the "primal world" time and time again. Only with great effort was I able to bring him back to the present. This manic encounter culminated in Nat wrapping his entire body round my favourite coffee table, a robust plastic affair, and crushing it to a mangled pulp. This display of raw, passionate emotion seemed to satisfy him and he came back to 1980 with a jolt.

I am glad that I was not the only one terrified by this extraordinary occurrence. Nat was clearly embarrassed at what he had done. Most of all, he was shocked at the very depths of seething emotion that lay beneath his usually unflappable lethargic facade.

I made some tea. We talked for a while and generally recuperated from the earlier excesses. As I drove Nat home, we both heard the church clock strike. We were greatly taken aback as, simultaneously and nonchalantly, we both glanced up at the moonlit tower. Slowly, we took in the fact that we'd been immersed in the regression session for the best part of three hours; it was eleven o'clock. I did not fear for Nat's safety on this occasion, for he was evidently too tired to do anything but sleep, soundly.

THU FEB 14

I saw Nat this morning. I attempted to gauge his depression, which is frequently at its height during this period of the day, as is common amongst sufferers of this illness. He was very morose, despite a good night's slumber. Indubitably, the primal therapy puts him in contact with the very core of his "sick" being. He said he had gained an insight. Life seemed less flat: it had "grown an extra dimension" after yesterday's struggles. I questioned him on this extra dimension and it seemed not wholly malignant. Still, I am wary of raising false hopes, for no sooner does Nat advance than he has a relapse.

Has not he noted, I wondered, throughout his life a steady development: from foetus to baby to child to youth to adult?

"To death", he added. Like all too many adolescents, he denies this pattern. He will not or cannot acknowledge his point blank refusal to grow up.

Surely it cannot be as simplistic as his comment suggests: namely, that adulthood is linked inexorably with death and must therefore be avoided.

SUN FEB 17

Nat went to see his friend Simeon in London yesterday. Simeon's continued browbeating of my patient resulted in a rather ugly incident. Nat, unable any longer to cope with his companion's verbal assault, involuntarily reverted to the foetal position. Thankfully he was able to pull out of it before unleashing any monstrous screams. Simeon had deliberately manipulated the scenario in order to provoke Nat's anger. This wasn't necessary, I told Nat.

From what Nat says, Simeon seems an interesting character, if somewhat misguided. His life is almost as bereft of emotional attachments as Nat's, but at least he gets out into the "real world" each day, even if it is—as he calls it—a "loonie-bin". Apparently, he got his information about primal therapy from a rather dubious second-hand source, and it centred on the work of Panov and the other Parisian experimental psychologists. Semidigested scraps of information can be so dangerous. The only positive thing to come out of the affair was that Nat had successfully made the train journey to South London and, even more remarkably, returned intact after the bout of impromptu regression. Very encouraging.

I made Nat telephone Simeon from my home—not an easy task—to let him know he had survived the minitrauma. Unaccountably, Simeon was totally unconcerned, I could hear him quite clearly shouting over the telephone. He had been confident that Nat would come to no harm. He would seem to be a rather angry young man.

Nat described Simeon's paintings. His work is greatly influenced by Lucian Freud, grandson of the great Sigmund, but also harks back to the symbolists. Fascinating though this was I let Nat know that, to me, "Simeon" is just a name.

MON FEB 18

In sympathy with current psychological theory, I do not find dreams "important"; they merely serve as a confusing glimpse of, or window onto, the subconscious and are open to infinite interpretations. Their primary function is a storing or filing of memory. The brain must stay active during sleep, and dreams serve as picturesque and often quite convincing entertainments. Their nature is quintessentially random.

Last night I dreamt that the earth was flat and that there were seas on the moon, which I could observe with ease through a purple-lensed telescope. A delicious dream.

On waking, quite stringent conscious efforts need to be made in order to recapture dreams. Popularisation of such procedures is becoming too haphazardly and unthinkingly commonplace. Dreams should only occupy one during the night-time; they do not function as things to be vexed over in the daylight hours. For five years now I have sought to obliterate my dreams, and much peace of mind it has brought me. Now, however, I intend to keep a record of them. I should like to extend meditation into my dreamworld, the most dangerous area one can explore as lucid dreaming seems to expunge the element of chance.

FRI FEB 22

Today I questioned Nat about his future. Is his life going to follow the path it is apparently locked into? For five years? Twenty years? What about when his parents eventually die? I told him that he is underachieving. He has a good brain and it would be a shame to waste it. He kept giggling most irritatingly. I decided it was time to terminate his sickness benefit, in a bid to make him fend for himself. Even if this should only force him into claiming unemployment benefit, that would be **something**, a gesture. He appeared so completely unmoved that I wondered, for one dreadful moment, if his whole illness had been feigned; an elaborate fabrication, concocted purely to humiliate me. He assured me that this was not the case, and I believe him. But most disconcertingly, he continued to cackle even after I had ushered him out of the room. From the window I watched him scuff down the High Street, heading straight for home. His parents told me that the only time he leaves the house is to see me. He did, however, see Simeon last week, but he never develops a string of engagements. He would probably make a most content inmate: the perfect prisoner, in fact.

I am in a dilemma. Nat is content for me to suggest what he should do with his life, but I am not sure what he wants. After all, his life has returned to its former pattern. He didn't see many people before I knew him. But this way of life had culminated in such drastic measures; or at least, his mother's efforts to get him out of his "shell", and his refusal to cooperate, had caused him to harm himself.

THUS FEB 28

I saw Nat and his parents today. For the best part of an hour we all bullied Nat. His parents feel he should go to college or take a job. Nat stubbornly refuses and has no shame in using emotional blackmail against them, usually thinly veiled threats of suicide should they push him too far. At the moment he still pays them his "keep" from the money he has saved from his sickness benefit, but this will not last forever. The most optimistic thing to emerge from the meeting was that Nat now seems more able to fight back, albeit in the most cruel and perverse manner. Nat's parents were overjoyed that he had successfully made the journey to and from London. They seem, unaware of what actually occurred at Simeon's, but still remain greatly in favour of the primal therapy, especially now that they have grown accustomed to it.

FRI FEB 29

I blatantly chastised Nat today for his behaviour towards his parents. If he insists on playing the precocious child, I will have to play the strict schoolmaster. He seems to hate his parents but he thinks he maintains a veneer of courtesy. I perceive a minimal change in him that is more permanent than his usual swings of mood. He is not so apathetic as he was. His appearance is somewhat neater but his teeth are a horrid green. I advised him to see his dentist. Of all the young people I have ever worked with, Nat's problems with approaching maturity are the most severe I have seen.

Last night I dreamt I was in a spacious echoing attic, with gigantic malodorous quenelles rolling about me making booming, rumbling sounds. I didn't feel in danger, and was able to take control of the dream. (See sex diary.)

MON MAR 3

It is one o'clock and I am very tired. This evening saw the third primal therapy session with Nat. As usual, I placed numerous cushions on the floor of my study. Nat relaxed quickly and I drew the curtains and turned out the light. He did not regress, despite my numerous proddings at his belly button. He was feeling nauseous and perceived a pain about the forehead. I applied pressure to the precise point of the cranium complaint with one hand whilst maintaining a hold and rhythmically massaging his stomach with the other. He reverted to the foetal position. Then came the screaming: grotesque glissandi culminating in shattering squalls on the highest notes. I maintained contact with him, continually pulling him back from the foetal world to find out what he was going through. At first he ceaselessly reenacted his suicide attempt, for the most part out of control and uninhibited. Gradually he began to gain glimpses -conscious insights into his behaviour. I told him we already knew about the slashed wrists, and he quietened down.

It seemed as though the session was over, when all of a sudden I became aware of Nat's mouth: it was wide open, his green teeth clearly visible as though lit from within. He began to emit morose groans and grim moans, then curled up tightly into a small ball. I turned on a reading lamp; the shock brought Nat firmly back into the present but only for a few seconds. Then he began screaming all over again, and clawed at his limbs, saying that he had no arms and legs, **just stumps**. The horrid expression on his face tallied all too well with such ugly utterances. Convinced he had an overview of the horrors that were unfolding, I allowed the session to continue. Nat squatted down in a corner then thrust his head up harshly against a bookcase. Manically, he lunged at me and would have attacked had he not abruptly grasped the gravity of what he was doing. Still, his countenance was one of malice, unmistakably aimed in my direction. Swiftly, his eyes settled upon my Buddha statuette and he rapidly assumed a full lotus position—such agility for one who never exercises!

Unfortunately, this phase didn't last long and Nat became abusive and generally obnoxious, adopting a most odd and unplaceable accent. I couldn't retrieve him from this state and he kept shouting "kill Nat" and pummelling the floor with his fists. He seemed to think he was in a padded cell. "It was a crime before Nat was born"; this was another memorable if baffling phrase which he kept crying.

This chilling performance finally lapsed into another extreme: he became a fawning namby pamby effeminate homosexual, of the music hall caricature type. Nat continued alternating between these various "characters" for so long and with so much energy that I could not get through to him. (There might be a paper in this, or at least a magazine article.)

In the end I had to call his father and one of my colleagues to help restrain him. At one point Nat escaped out of the front door, heedlessly scuttling barefoot over the wet grass. Fortunately he was in his mincing mode and we were soon able to round him up and take him home.

I tried to administer a sedative but by now his arms were flailing and he was screaming again. I couldn't locate a vein. He squealed. I made a right pig's ear of it, covering his arms in bruises and almost gave up the idea of an intravenous tranquiliser, but eventually I succeeded and he soon calmed down for real, indeed becoming very woozy. His parents were very helpful.

TUE MAR 4

Before going to the surgery I looked in on Nat to ensure he was "himself". I made a time to see him later in the day and explained to his parents what had happened the night before, even though I still don't fully understand it myself.

Nat arrived late for our appointment; only five minutes late, but nonetheless unheard of for him. The reason? His body ached all over from the frenzies of the regression session; yes, and so did mine.

How could he explain what he had experienced, the different "characters"? He was hasty to discount reincarnation, but he did expound a reasonably intelligent theory. Namely, that the "characters" were merely personifications of his own repressed "traits", as it were, with fragments of information recalled from the subconscious.

It is important, in psychoanalysis, to take into account the patient's interpretation of events. Here, however, I think that Nat's concept is as good as any. Therefore I attempted to question Nat about these various "traits". He said he did not understand them and refused to speak, resorting to his infuriating cackling. He was almost hyperventilating. I had to change tack. The violent crazed man he became; could it have been a "ghost" from his childhood? His parents were sure they didn't know of anyone like it when I had questioned them last night. I put this to Nat. He was fairly shocked by the notion, as if his theory was the most logical, and therefore true. I told him how offensive I found the stereotyped effeminate homosexual, but he just tittered. I am still finding difficulty working out just what his smiles and laughter mean. They don't seem to be a purely nervous reaction, but anxiety is the emotion that comes most to mind when one thinks of Nathaniel Snoxell.

I wondered if Nat's aggression had been directed at me; not me personally, but at my role as a catalyst in Nat's life. He confessed to having felt this in the therapy session but saw it as irrational in the clear light of day.

When working intimately with patients I invariably develop loving feelings for them. This is the case with Nat and I divulged this to him. I am happy to say, he confided in me that he was not unaware of his own loving feelings for me. In the past I have had to be scrupulously careful with young people, as they have regularly and openly sought my affections. The opposite is true with Nat, who would appear to be the perfect prude.

TUE MAR 11

Nat's mood remains dark and sombre. I advised him to go out for a walk each day. This he has promised to undertake.

Last night I dreamt of a frightful house, constructed entirely from nerves and veins. Numerous were the heads growing from the sides of the walls and from the floorboards, each one flinging itself about madly, deliberately attempting to crick its neck. I was able to steer the dream into gentler imagery. It would seem that years of dreamworld forgetfulness have taken their toll on me. I was not prepared for the bad taste the dream left, haunting me throughout the day. Its source would appear to be last week's primal session with Nat, and a particularly severe case of haemorrhoids which I treated a few days later.

TUE MAR 18

Nat has been following my suggested walking regime and seems the better for it, if only superficially. He firmly believes that the weakest bodies create the sickliest thoughts, therefore if I goad him into physical fitness this may in turn have a placebo effect, as it were, on his depression. Nat was almost overwhelmed with amazement when I pointed out that, if he were to put his mind to it, he could easily be stronger than me. Detecting a hint of malicious glee forming in his normally dull eyes, I let him know that—should he care to try it—he will have a fight on his hands.

WED MAR 19

Today included a tiresome, tedious session with that boy Snoxell and his parents. We went over and over the same old ground, getting nowhere. In desperation I almost mentioned his secret cellar and neurotic attic, but resisted the temptation: such a revelation at this stage could only rupture the gradually improving relations between the parents and their problem child. Nat's family cannot be expected to understand his situation. Why, they don't even have an inkling of what he is going through. They weren't happy with his life before he made clear his suicidal designs, but at least he "kept busy" then. Small wonder they think he is shirking, or perceive his mysterious malady to be merely "madness".

These group sessions have served their purpose now: even Nat is becoming immune to their embarrassment value. I see no reason why they should continue.

TUE MAR 25

I told Nat of my decision to cease the work with his parents. He was much more relieved than I had anticipated. "You didn't like it at all, did you, Nat?" He shook his head, quite vigorously by his standards. Perhaps I have been too hasty here; I shall certainly bear in mind the possibility of future impromptu parental assemblies. Nat looked, in general, quite happy, but still talked of dark things.

SUN MAR 30

Another primal therapy session with Nat. This followed the earlier patterns of rapid regressions and sinister screams. His hair is now so long that I kept having to brush it out of his face in order to study his expression. After one particularly searing scream, seemingly made with his **whole body**, he came to with a shudder.

He spoke fanatically, as only the young can, of the scream's significance. He had **been** the creation of the universe; the moment when the human egg is fertilised and begins to spin, **whole**. Not only did he lay claim to the Alpha, but he also annexed the Omega: he **was** the cosmic collapse. My disbelief was suspended by his undoubted sincerity. Slightly caught up in his enthusiasm I suggested that he had experienced a brief snatch of Nirvana, which is what one attempts to attain through meditation. On reflection, awesome though Nat's experience was, it seemed to go straight from birth to death as if the two were directly related, with nothing between the two extremes. "Foetal enlightenment" is well documented in primal therapy literature, but I have found nothing yet that really matches what Nat described.

Despite his excitement, or because of it, we were quickly able to resume the business in hand. And yet it seemed Nat's concentration had gone, for when he opened his mouth only a tiny high-pitched squeal came out, then nothing. Later I discovered some hair line cracks on my study window. A mother and her offspring, whilst it is growing inside her, can communicate ultrasonically. Surely it is ridiculous to surmise that Nat's feeble squallings caused the miniscule faults in the glass? I was just becoming accustomed to this anticlimax, when Nat suddenly began to slam his head with frightening ferocity against the floor. So unexpected and rapid were his movements that he managed to carry out this sickening and manic manoeuvre three or four times before I could place a cushion between the floor and his head. I made him aware of what he was doing. The activity continued, but with much less ferocity. For half an hour he rolled about the floor; by turns violent, passive, agitated and violent once more. Gently but firmly I placed my hands around his neck.

"How does that feel?" I asked.

"Stuck", came the revealing reply.

The session was over. Nat eagerly discussed the proceedings, clearly greatly stimulated by the turn of events. When I was satisfied that he had calmed down sufficiently I took him home. For once my evening engagements were not interfered with.

The material produced during the primal therapy sessions with Nat is of a most erratic nature. The treatment is not noted for producing a chronologically perfect sequence of events from the first few months of life, but equally Nat's flitting about from one stage of development to another is hardly the norm. This could be due to the violence of the material, i.e. that it is just too painful for his conscious mind to tolerate the suffering of those days gone by.

So far I have refrained from studying the birth notes in the case of Nathaniel Snoxell, for fear that they might prejudice my findings. Now, however, I feel a perusal of them would be most beneficial, along with a discussion with my senior colleagues who brought Nat into the world and who wrote those self-same notes.

MON MAR 31

I saw Nat today. He is looking well but still has deathly thoughts. I acquainted him with my brand new theory—in simplified form of course—namely that whilst he was being born he became "stuck" and believed he was dying, or wanted to die, to stop the pain. This "death wish" then lingered partly subdued throughout his life until once more his mother innocently attempted to push him into the outside world. This seemingly benign action resulted in bringing down upon him all the repressed death feelings, in a single torrent. Oval Wood was the "womb" in which he had unknowingly reenacted this first trauma, once again coming desperately close to death but emerging just in time.

Nat was totally unimpressed, as though he had envisaged something altogether more grand. I told him that nothing unusual had happened during his birth according to my senior colleague, the doctor in charge at Nat's birth. What he remembered mostly was "that ghostly house" into which the Snoxells had then only fairly recently installed themselves, and that Nat had been born on the stroke of midnight; notes made at the time confirmed this.

The doctor is a practitioner of the old school and had never fully considered, until I questioned him, the effects birth has on a person's character. Surprisingly enough, it was his experience that the more difficult the birth the more well-balanced the person seemed to become. "Blue babies", who only just survived, went on to become active and respected members of the community, whereas those with "easy" births lived dull lives. I didn't like what he was inferring here; had he forgotten I was born by caesarean section? And yet he concluded by stating that he saw all this as purely coincidental, the character being decided before birth. Problems don't count per se. What is essential is the individual's ability and willingness to overcome them.

Nat was more than a little stunned by this somewhat brusque analysis. He had clearly fantasised an alternative birth scenario for himself, which he would not divulge. It was not just his rejection of my theory, or the look on his face, but I intuitively feel that Nat has some "unfinished business". Perhaps I was asking a little much by requiring Nat to rationalise his feelings so as to fit neatly into the water-tight compartment of my theory. He did concede that my "explanation" was logical and agreed to contemplate it more seriously. I never really expected Nat to go waltzing out of the surgery, a happy man. I had however predicted that some glimmer of recognition might light up his face, however temporarily.

WED APR 2

Nat remains unmoved by my theory. Still, it is only a theory. I told him of my latest musings regarding his drawings: that they could be expressions of his experience of birth. The grotesque, warped distorted heads: surely how most babies perceive what is happening to them when they are being born, what with their own skulls still malleable. And yet Nat had drawn these pictures before I had ever mentioned primal therapy. Had they been a premonition of my diagnosis?

When I saw them I was left with the very powerful impression that Nat has a far greater insight into what he was doing than is granted to most artists. Enragingly, he refused to speak, but by the angle at which he held his head, I could tell he was feeling decidedly smug.

What was he doing here? The philosophy currently being popularised in contemporary fiction, that psychoanalysis, whilst often "curing" a patient of antisocial behaviour, also strips away individuality and visionary insight, suddenly struck me as utterly nonsensical. The patient gets what the patient wants.

And what does Nat want?
"I don't know".

FRI APR 4

I dropped by at Nat's gloomy house today. It was ages before he came to the door. He offered me tea but, as I am trying to cut down my caffeine addiction, I had to refuse.

I asked him if he had been doing any drawing. "A bit", by which he meant up to three hours a day. Quite a lot, really.

I coaxed him into showing me a few of the macerated specimens. His subject matter had changed from heads to foetuses. They are unlike the vaguely demoniac embryos seen in Odilon Redon or Aubrey Beardsley's work, said to have been inspired, in Redon's case, by the artist and his sister performing an abortion on their own baby. Rather, they are frightful, disfigured creatures with no control over their existences, leading horrific sublives, wrought from Nat's own experience with which primal therapy had put him in contact. One picture was particularly engrossing: a vortex of violent volutes, with voodoo babies and foetuses banging their heads against brick walls. Some of these offspring looked far too intelligent, like mad professors, but this illusion was caused by their circular spectacle-like eyes and high embryonic foreheads.

I told Nat that I had been in contact with Dr. Blitzein, a Scot of Germanic ancestry, and the country's leading expert on regression and primal therapy. Blitzein had shown some interest in the Snoxell case and as I imparted this information to Nat his countenance took on the mingled pride and self-disgust of the Victorian circus freak one knows so well from early photographs. Nat could hardly hide his joy that his life should warrant such illustrious attention: he has always thought that he is special. I asked him if I could borrow the "foetal-vortex" picture for photocopying, in order to allow Blitzein to peruse the imagery. Under the circumstances, Nat seemed only too pleased to oblige. He gave me an old school file to carry the piece away in.

WED APR 9

Blitzein was not too impressed with Nat's drawing. Perhaps it lost something in the mechanical reproduction process. The photocopy I sent to him **was** a little blurred. Still his curiosity was sufficiently roused—in a "sanitarium of art" manner—to phone me this morning. His interest lies at the very frontiers of medicine and not with its social applications. He went along with my theory about Oval Wood being a symbolic womb where, due to "emotional pressure", Nat had reenacted what he had experienced as a violent birth. Blitzein suggested that there might be something in Nat's recent history, more tenable than "emotional pressure", which had led to the suicide attempt. He wasn't surprised to hear about Nat's gruesome collection of weird things. However, he spent most of our telephone conversation speculating on Russian embryo experiments, about which he has heard bleak rumours. We concluded that Nat seemed to have some unfinished business and a few more regression sessions might clear up the case.

FRI APR 11

I returned Nat's picture. He went straight for the one miniscule crease I had accidentally made in it, and I had to apologise profusely. He still seemed quite excited about Blitzein although I didn't raise that subject. I tried to question him once more about sexuality, and yet again this proved futile. Not everyone can discuss sex, even in this day and age. I don't think that there's anything seriously amiss with the youth. He may just have a low sex drive, or more likely be a "late developer", to use the words of his mother. Nat does not actively denounce the erotic principle, but rather has channelled his energies into weirdness: into staving off or indulging in "doom-laden" feelings, and into his macabre dabblings.

TUE APR 15

The fifth primal session with Nat. Early evening. It took him a long time to become relaxed. Eventually he curled up tight, into a ball. And then came the screaming which, for once, caught me unawares, because it was quite normal. He continually threw himself about the floor, whilst I softened his painful path by discreetly placing cushions at the salient points. Just as it seemed that this mode of behaviour would last the whole session, he stretched out. His previously tightly shut eyes began to twitch and he snatched glimpses of my head and torso silhouetted by the setting sun, towering over his prostrate body. Suddenly he began to wince and shun my form. I asked him what he perceived this to mean. No reply. He continued wincing. This was interspersed occasionally with short, more relaxed periods until the end of the session. Usually it is me that determines the session's termination point, but this time Nat just sat bolt upright, fully awake.

Nat was able to verbalise his experience. He simply felt he could not tolerate the presence of a lurking figure. He knew perfectly well it was not my small frame that had made him so fearful and that dual consciousness had supplied him with a traumatic memory. Nat traced this horrific recollection to the one day he had spent in a nursery run by nuns. I think that this memory dates from further back, but not as far back as birth. When he had returned from the nursery, he had begged his parents never to send him again to those "witches". He had mentioned this to me before, but I had forgotten.

WED APR 16

I dropped in at Nat's between house calls, to ensure that he had not suffered any adverse effects from yesterday's trip into his formative era. He seemed okay, but it's hard to tell. Certainly his dental hygiene has improved, and consequently his smile was pleasing; less of a baring of teeth in animal aggression—the green grin, as I called it—than of late. He looks well, still persisting with the walks, even if they do centre around the churchyard. At least he doesn't appear to spend so much time in his awful aumbries, although he remains reticent on this topic.

FRI APR 18

I dreamt of a primaeval landscape, which disturbingly quickly metamorphosed into lush, rolling, quintessentially **English** countryside, of the variety which everyone seems to carry around in their heads but which has never really existed, nor is it now ever likely to exist. Curious sproutings of green fungi incongruously began to blemish the pastoral idyll. Huge butterflies swooped from nowhere, their movements corresponding so precisely with accompanying high-pitched pipe music that I imagined they must have studied elaborate choreographies whilst in their chrysalises. This anthropomorphism seems utterly ridiculous now, as is so often the case with dreams.

This fanciful musing apparently found a strong resonance in the dream, for it became clear to me that the wings of the lepidopterous insects did not display the expected colourful patterns, pretty patches, speckles and spots, no: each butterfly's organs of flight contained a single, symmetrical face. At first the flying faces were expressionless, but then they began to squeal, like dog whistles. The features on two of the winged creatures I recognised as my own and those of Nathaniel Snoxell.

The dream alarmed me. I was immensely relieved when I found I was gaining control of it. I gently dreamt of an ancient city that gave the impression of having been built by artists and sculptors. Slender, tapering chryselephantine towers pierced chromospheric clouds in a vortex of shattering kaleidoscopes. Stained glass domes, illuminated from within, painted the sky with glorious images. The honeyed air held me spellbound, whilst magical music, similar to Javanese orchestras but much more delicate and subtle, enchanted my ears. I have no idea from where such quaint picturesqueness springs—perhaps from an overindulgence in florid fiction during my student days. The accompanying fires of love feelings were, however, genuine.

WED APR 23

Nat's mother is "heckling" him, as he puts it, into going to college or taking a job. I hate to think what kind of a job someone of eighteen with no experience could get. He shares my view that manual labour would be soul-destroying, but I do support Mrs. Snoxell's efforts in steering him towards college. I told her that I am sure Nat will take up the reins of normal life when he is ready. I said to Nat that I could just see him as a tramp in a few years' time. He was shocked but soon recovered his poise, unfortunately.

SUN APR 27

I had a dream with controlled relaxational material. All of a sudden the pleasantries ceased and crumbled in front of my "eyes". It was like watching a favourite painting crack and decay into dust—a process which normally takes centuries—encapsulated within a few seconds. Then I was aware of hurling around an energy force at an incredible velocity, like a manic planet around its sun. I certainly felt globular. Then I began to see myself as a stationary **single eyeball**, with all-perfect but condensed human physiology held within. The exception was that I had no personality, making me the epitome of a voyeur as I beheld the scene unfolding.

I began to remember my earlier dreams; before I'd sought forgetfulness of all nocturnal sleeping visions, and where I had been the centre of both attention and action. The dream acquiesced.

Still disembodied, I observed "myself" regressing Nat. Everything was going well, until Nat began to **melt**, dissolving into amniotic fluid, semen and female sex secretions. I was able to halt the imagery—which I found horrific—but the respite was all too brief. I found myself ensnared within a glass dome surrounded by an orange haze. As far as I could see, there was row upon row of similar structures each containing one, or on occasion two, knotted and furled pink figures. Gradually and grotesquely it dawned on me that in the dome opposite me was the foetal form of Nathaniel Snoxell, his features rudimentary but unmistakable. My deliquescent friend had metamorphosed once more. We were in foetid formaldehyde jars. With immense concentration, I dreamt happily of friends, so successfully that I obliterated the "nightmare". Almost.

WED APR 30

Today was Nat's birthday. He doesn't seem like a person of nineteen. At least his life is not so "baby-like" as it was before we started the primal therapy. He gets out of the house each day and keeps busy with his drawing. He is far less nocturnal now. I do not think that he is, or ever has been agoraphobic, but just needs constant rousing to prevent him underachieving. I simply cannot believe Nat when he says that he is "lazy": the recent artwork he has shown me, and his strict adherence to a well-balanced vegan diet, resolutely disprove such a myth.

MON MAY 5

I dropped by again at Nat's today. He said he'd had his hair cut. "Oh, which one?" I asked. He didn't laugh.

His mother told me that he has asked her to buy him a guitar—an acoustic one. She didn't seem enthusiastic until I demonstrated my approval. Any activity, however noisy, is helpful. "Be thankful it's not amplified", I suggested.

TUE MAY 13

Nat rather sheepishly confessed to having acquired an acoustic guitar. He became even more uneasy when I informed him that I already knew. The fingers on his left hand were raw, so eager is he to learn, and he has even overcome the beginner's bane of sustaining a chord. Although at the moment he only aspires to long drone-ridden dirges, I believe that his fascination for the instrument will eventually educe much more beneficial effects, most of them probably not musical.

I fixed a time for another primal therapy session. Nat didn't feel it was necessary, but I persuaded him.

MON MAY 19

The sixth regression session with Nathaniel Snoxell. The foetal position was quickly assumed. His rictus was elongated almost to the point of jaw dislocation. Ghastly screams tapered off most unexpectedly into a mild sigh. Behaviours of the previous session were repeated: shunning my form with face distorted into an expression of utter panic; needing to express terror of the whole body which remained limp and inactive. Nat then felt very sad. I could not comfort him. He did not want to be held or hugged. It seems he cannot reach the point of tearful release of repressed sufferings from before and during birth: one of the most vital constituents of primal therapy. He skipped this phase entirely and went into a gentle repose with minimal finger movements that he later described as "writing".

I am still baffled as to what actually caused the panic in the first place. I took Nat home. He was in a good mood. The session had lasted nearly an hour.

TUE MAY 20

I discussed with Nat the implications of last night's work. He was fascinated by the display of raw fear, quite unlike anything that he has ever seen in film, fiction or art. Nat is gleeful that I have yet to come up with a suitable theory to match his behaviour.

He is persevering with the guitar. His younger brother is offering him musical advice but he only accepts perverse snatches of music theory. Tritones—the infamous "Devil's Tone"—are a particular obsession. He retunes the guitar to his own desires. The neighbours don't seem to mind this, but do take exception to the occasional wild vocal improvisations which are liberally sprinkled with screams.

TUE MAY 27

Nat has developed an intense fear of the dark. Most phobias are now generally reckoned to stem from a feeling of imminent death during birth. This fear, being too painful to recall in later life, latches itself onto something less significant but no less frightening. When patients are shown just how irrational their fears are (of spiders, open spaces, crowds etc. etc.), the fears often miraculously "vanish". This therapy is in my opinion not wholly effective in that it fails to deal with the **cause** of the fear.

I attempted to treat Nat's dread of the dark by this rationalising approach. It has had some effect. Nat now investigates any objects in his benighted bedroom which engender his terror. Once he is convinced that the objects are in order, the fear loses much of its ferocity. However, Nat's house is so ghoulish that I am not entirely convinced that his fear **is** irrational. Ergo I have also advised him to turn out his concealed loft-tomb. This he was loath to do, but he seemed pleased that I had connected this with his fright.

SAT MAY 31

I am glad to say that the scars on Nat's wrists are healing nicely. He is not, as he should be, ashamed of them, but contrariwise seems quite proud. This is not the pride of a battle-scarred war veteran, but a sort of **wicked** pride. I think it may well be time for some more therapy.

SUN JUN 1

I have just completed a long-winded, tedious regression session with Nat. He kept giggling during the relaxation stage, especially when tightening and releasing the muscles in his buttocks. I tried to ignore such childish jests and sniggers, saying it was okay to laugh and the more he laughed the more he would become relaxed. To my amazement, this worked. Actually, he became so relaxed that it seemed a shame to take him back to more troubled times. Indeed, only after considerable hectoring did he assume the foetal position. He emitted no screams, merely whiffled and whined and, aside from a panic attack familiar from the last two sessions, there was no violence. Most of the time was spent with his body splayed out in total abandon, with just his right hand "conscious" making the spidery movements which he still insists on calling writing, although he cannot discern the text. He was mildly elated after the session, having experienced euphoria and a more permanent sense of well-being during it. Sadly this was not evident from the outside, for Nat was not displaying any easy-to-interpret signals.

I drove Nat home. In the car he speculated on what he had been "writing". Most of it, as far as he could tell, was the "literary equivalent of gibberish". Occasionally he gained an insight into what he was writing and he felt it to be terribly profound.

MON JUN 2

I saw Nat today. The usual routine. I checked he was all right in the wake of another hour of regression. He seems very bored by the whole affair now. I persisted in discussing the matter with him, because I think it is important. I suggested that he had been scared in his cradle, which would account for his panic attacks in recent sessions. This shred of theoretical information stimulated his imagination. However, I find the idea much more mundane: any number of things could have frightened the infant Nat, so intrinsically **weird** is the house where he was born and still lives. I stressed that both events, the "bad birth" and the possible disturbance in early infancy, actually happened **nearly twenty years ago**.

Perhaps, I suggested, he should take a broader perspective and not allow them so much influence over his present state of being, recognition of the problem being half the cure. Nat heard me out but I could tell that he was trying to espy in his mind's eye just **what** exactly had scared him in his cradle.

WED JUN 4

I have sufficient confidence in Nat to leave him for two weeks whilst I take my holiday.

THU JUN 5

I sent Nat a postcard. Told him to be good.

WED JUN 18

I arrived home to find that Nat had returned my compliment: he had sent me a postcard, in a perfect act of sarcasm, of Black Langley. He had even scrawled a greeting and message about the weather using the self same shade of purple felt pen that I favour!

FRI JUN 20

I saw Nat; we exchanged pleasantries. I thanked him for the postcard; he thanked me for mine. Yes, I had had a nice time. He had survived okay without me—even flourished. Over the last two weeks Nat has been trying to form a **band**. What on earth prompted such drastic action? Had he missed me after all? While the cat's away. . .

Acute boredom had forced him to such an extreme. A friend of his younger brother had put him in touch with a bass guitarist, who is fifteen years old and goes by the name of Greg. He has a hare lip, cleft palate and other malformations. Nat ungraciously calls him "Freak", but they seem to get along well enough. Greg is obsessed by "punk" music of the last decade. I had thought it extinct by now, or at least out of fashion. The punk styles have been transmuted, absorbed and adopted by society, though the polemics—always a minority taste—remain untouched.

Nat informed me that "punk is not a fashion, it's an attitude". I have heard this somewhere before. I must say I am relieved that both he and Greg take this view and will not be resorting to the war-zone dress sense of many punks. Nat gleefully described the "corpse of punk" as having no life in it whatsoever, and it was this decayed grandeur of a fallen subculture which had so attracted him.

I let him know at the outset that I can in no way relate to punk. He intimated that it was the same story with his parents. "It's just their generation" he said; "at least they've got an excuse!" But like me, they are pleased that Nat is at last taking an interest in the outside world, however warped that interest might be.

WED JUN 25

Despite Nat's new-found hobby, he still suffers with his death wish fixation, although he often denies its existence, and on such occasions cannot explain where the doom-laden feelings have gone. However, I am convinced his overall mood is changing from despair and blackness to a subtle mixture of melancholy, an aching for what has been and what is to come, and an authentic but harrowing form of déjà vu. His efforts to convey this complex set of impressions and emotions found a resonance in me, for he managed to communicate his feelings perfectly, although they include things for which our language has no words. The way he got his ideas across was most memorable. For the most part he employed gestures of the head, but the phrases "life golden sad" and "hyper-manqué" also stay with me.

Nat is beginning to accept the fact that his doom-laden emotions will never fully disappear. With more work, however, we can hope to lessen their domination of his personality. Naturally, he finds it rather dubious to desire to dispel something which has been so large a part of him throughout his life. He tends towards the light but darkness pulls him back. I wish I could give him a pill that would provide the thrill and insight of his love of death, whilst simultaneously freeing him from the threat that it poses to his life. Such a pill, sadly, does not exist, and psychology favours all-pervasive healthy normalcy over morbid unwholesomeness, however visionary it might be.

TUE JUL 1

Nat and his friend Greg are having difficulty finding a drummer for their band. This is hardly surprising, as Greg has named the band—using a smattering of his 0-level studies in biology—after the androgynous human embryo's undeveloped genitalia. His grasp of Latin is atrocious. Nat is amused by it and seems to relish the embarrassing nature of the band's name. Greg had formulated the name before even meeting Nat, let alone hearing of his primal therapy experiences.

The two youths are already close. Greg is a vegetarian and so shares at least this one life-affirming characteristic with Nat. He also has pretensions to anarchism and feminism, but essentially the main similarity is an indulgence in the macabre. Wisely, Greg is going to stay on at school for the sixth form. They talk for hours about their "illnesses": Greg has had many operations for his condition and still needs some more cosmetic surgery. Their relationship seems to be exclusive, Greg being shunned by his classmates and regularly harangued and heckled in the street. Exclusive relationships can always be dangerous, particularly when they dwell upon the negative. I therefore recommended to Nat a well-balanced young man of my acquaintance: a serious student of music, but also an avid player of the drums. But Nat was not interested when he found the prospective candidate had no interest in punk.

MON JUL 7

Nat has found a drummer for his band, someone he knew vaguely at school called Jim to whom he refers as "Imbecile". I am content to overlook his prejudices whilst his outside interests are gaining momentum. Actually as one of Nat's former friends (a general practice patient of mine) pointed out, "in these days of super-egalitarianism Nat's comments serve as a welcome corrective".

Greg is unhappy with the new recruit. Skilled as Jim is, having mastered, Nat tells me, the basic techniques at the age of seven, he does not share Nat's political ideals and, horror of horrors, is not even a vegetarian. He prefers to spend his time when not rehearsing consuming alcohol and meat pies (he only eats meat), down the pub. Nat and Greg are also ambivalent about having someone of such professional stature within the band: Jim does session work for several local commercial groups. It seems enthusiasm and raw energy are the essential ingredients of punk music and Greg is somewhat hypocritical in his denouncements, as he has been having bass lessons for over a year. Therefore the band rely on Nat's shouting and screaming and elementary but weird guitar "antistyle" to supply them with an authentic punk sound.

Last week Nat bought an electric guitar and something called a "fuzz-box" which distorts the sound (as if an electric guitar wasn't distortion enough!) Jim supplies the rest of the equipment and they practice at his house. Greg and Nat are ferried there and back by their parents. Some anarchists!

Still, the image of Nat releasing anger in this way is far more acceptable than mutilating his body. He does seem to have a lot of pent-up anger that comes out during his writing and playing of "songs". Indeed, the very idiom he uses indicates this. Punk, after all, is a music of hatred and destruction, but it is still **music**, i.e. a statement of hope not pessimism. Nat does not see it as an adequate catharsis. Indeed, he does not believe in catharsis. He does believe in some things: evocation of certain moods—predominantly bizarre—in his lyrics and drawings. He spoke at great length about his humble ambitions for the band, putting me quite behind schedule with my other appointments, but it was worth it.

THU JUL 15

I have just had what is likely to be the last primal therapy session with Nat. It was almost a facsimile of the previous two and, as per usual, was held in my study. Only a single incident differed: at one point he stood up and, with great aplomb, picked out the only book of about two thousand that doesn't belong to me! A dilapidated tome, a questionable study of anatomy lent to me in my student days—it was ancient even then. The rest of the session, almost two hours, Nat spent simply lying on the floor. There were occasional movements of his hands which he still insists is a type of writing.

WED JUL 16

I asked Nat: "Where do we go from here?" He seemed devastated at the prospect of no longer seeing me. As far as I can tell there is little more I can do for him. The primal therapy has helped him understand his feelings and recently he has become a lot less isolated. I had to admit that I do like seeing him and I have agreed to continue with our meetings, though I think this may be a mistake.

SAT JUL 19

I dreamt of a giant bird's nest—something from childhood fairy tales. A roc perhaps? It was filled with butchered babies. Some were skeletons; these ones were **moving** and **screaming**. Unbearable. Then I was assailed by equally repulsive imagery: the large door of a massive oven-incinerator-cauldron swung open and pieces of human beings were spewed out, mainly huge tracts of bluish-tinged gut, but then cancerous brains and all manner of human garbage. All this material then assembled, or rather reassembled itself into a sizeable army of zombies. Not since dissection days have I suffered such nightmares. Probably they were induced by Nat's discovery of that borrowed book.

The dream, or nightmare, seemed just like reality. I was not even aware of it being a dream. I saw a programme on television just a few days ago which covered all the latest developments in lucid dreaming. I was suddenly struck by just how primitive even the most advanced research is. I fear that lucid dreaming may be a form of censorship. One must face horrors in dreams.

THU JUL 24

Nat has recovered his poise a little after my sudden declaration that the usefulness of our meetings had come to an end. He has even taken action and signed on the dole! This was against his principles, he insisted, but he has done it in order to "have more money for the band". Perhaps I should threaten the boy more often!

Nat goes almost every evening now to see Greg. They rehearse new material and practice their earlier efforts. Apparently Nat went to many punk concerts in his early teens and understands the subculture well. He is adamant that he went along as an "observer of degenerates"—he never actually spoke to anyone. Greg is educating him with regard to recent developments, or regressions in the genre. They rarely go out for the evening, but instead listen incessantly to Greg's comprehensive collection of punk records. They also study "fanzines", the literature of the subcult. Greg wants a spikey-haired singer in the band, but Nat resists this. His hair is becoming long again and he insists that his material should be sung only by himself. I must admit to being a little apprehensive about Nat's band ever playing before an audience, mode of dress and style being the essential qualifications for entry into any tribe.

I asked Nat if he objected to me writing up his case for the medical journals. Her seemed quite excited. I told him Blitzein had suggested it, because not much has been written about primal therapy in Britain, and cultural differences may result in nuances from country to country. Nat was quite happy for me to write about him. I explained that I would naturally change all the relevant names and locations, i.e. the wood etc. I also gave him my permission to document the events should he ever feel compelled to do so. I gained the impression that he would like to read my papers but I do not think that this would be beneficial.

MON JUL 28

Nat has been complaining about a vivid fear of Oval Wood, and a railway bridge which he has to go under at night when returning home from Greg's. Actually I think it is "photophobia", or rather a **love of fear** which is the matter with Nat. Last night I took him to these places in my car and he pointed out the "fearful shadows" and "odd shapes" that so terrify him beneath the railway bridge. I could see nothing scary and advised him to go up to the shadows and convince himself of their benignity, as he had done previously with the objects that horrified him at night in his bedroom. This eased his fear but he complained that he still felt panic. I said that he would probably never dispel this fear entirely, but that he is certainly capable of keeping it at a tolerable level.

We went on up to Oval Wood on foot, the track being ruinous to machinery. Nat's fantasy fear here was that an evil nun lurked menacingly behind a tree, waiting for him. We found no such thing, so Nat pointed out that the towering trees had **faces** in their branches. I could not share this illusion. We went into the wood itself, and after a while Nat became calm and somewhat more at ease in the dark.

Ironically, on the way back to the car a fierce dog followed us, snapping at our heels. I had to confess to Nat my mild phobia of dogs. He was intrigued to hear how, when I was three years old, I was pushed to the ground and worried by an Alsatian—I do not think that Nat had ever envisioned me as a child before! He muttered something about "the refracting glass of psychology", and suggested that, if all contributors to rational medical science were irrational, would it not be logical to assume irrational elements in the treatments that they formulated? He gloated over this mischievous concept whilst my pulse quickened, in fear of the dog.

WED JUL 30

I dreamt of vast prisms; visions of vivid schisms. Infinite whirling vortex of time and space, with self, still, at the centre. Zen Buddhist wish fulfilment!

WED AUG 6

Nat's band have got a "gig". He seems to like my adoption of the jargon though he seldom favours it himself. They will play along with several other local groups, at a church hall in Black Langley in a few weeks' time. Nat is disdainful of the whole affair, but I continue to impress upon him that he has to start somewhere. Greg took it upon himself to get them involved. Jim, for his sins, will be playing in at least two of the bands. He does not seem at all perturbed by this; indeed it is Nat and Greg who are most apprehensive. I hope it goes well for them: any positive experience where Nat is concerned must be therapeutic.

THU AUG 14

Nat is still being quite disturbed by the dark. Invariably this happens after studying some obscure art form or reading macabre literature. I advised him to lay off such indulgences well before bedtime. Paradoxically, he showed no mistrust of the night during his “nocturnal phase”, or in those nasty niches of his which he calls his “cubby-holes”, implying cosiness. They would terrify most people, but he finds them soothing, probably due to familiarity. Personally I think that the trepidation stems from his emergence into the real world, not from any fear of the dark.

WED AUG 20

I dropped in at Nat’s. His parents seem quite excited about the forthcoming concert. They overcame their doubts once they saw that their second son had not pierced his nose with a safety pin. They were, however, somewhat alarmed at Nat’s plan to wear a grotesque mask for the performance. I subsequently managed to talk him out of this: his confidence will not be boosted by the gig unless he can fully face the audience. This is the best chance we have to abate his fear of crowds, for he has refused help for this phobia in the past.

THU AUG 28

Nat and his band survived their baptism into the world of subcultural “show-business”. After familiarising him with my own experience of “live work” I asked him if he felt nervous before or after the concert. He said both, and I let him know my verdict: I believe him to be an **anxiety addict**. However, it was Greg who shook the most, adding an unintentional vibrato to his playing, doubtless inaudible beneath the combined barrage of drums, guitar and vox.

The audience was comprised, chiefly, of brothers and sisters of the artists, but none of Nat’s family attended. Several younger adolescents were a little disturbed by Nat’s histrionics: one was even sick. (Perhaps Nat should have worn a mask after all. I presented this jokey notion to him; he groaned.) Nat was greatly saddened that he wasn’t able to recreate the monstrous screams that were such an outstanding feature of our primal therapy work. I advised that he should not persist in this misguided quest. Regression in public, however fantastic or spectacular a piece of magical showmanship it might be, could be immensely hazardous. He pondered the question. It had obviously only been a whim, and he proceeded to succinctly outline the disastrous consequences such ill-considered behaviour would entail.

Nat was quite delighted that the local constabulary had shown a good deal of interest in the concert. He felt that the arrest of a youth during a minor fracas for dislodging a policeman's helmet had set the seal of approval, or rather disapproval on the band's first outing, in spite of the fact that the youth was later released uncharged. He only heard of this incident a little while after the gig, through Jim. His life still seems predominantly **vicarious**.

FRI SEP 5

Nat is very unhappy with the music his band is making. "Why not change it then?" I asked.

He says he can't. The reality seems not to match the ideal.

I insisted that we all have to cope with this problem. I was so moved by his plight that I told him of mine: whether or not to give up medicine and enter the back-stabbing world of the professional violinist. He seemed most concerned. I said that I could still see him, but his concern went deeper than that. He seemed quite stunned to find me in such a quandary, as if he were the only one subject to human foibles and the rest of us were **aliens**. Nat hoped he wasn't a contributory factor to my present dilemma. I assured him that he was not.

WED SEP 10

I had a particularly foul dream. I was aware that it was a dream, and I could influence its direction but chose not to. A tall thin youth (an ignis fatuus, it turned out) was walking down a rickety road. His limbs suddenly went completely out of control, like wild crazy concertinas, or mad elastic. He then continued on his way unabated. That was all. The most singular aspect of the dream was its **mood**, for it was accompanied by a most wonderful sense of well-being. Indeed, not until long after it was over did this feeling diminish and the horrific implications of the repulsive imagery fully strike home.

This, as far as I can recall, is my only dream to exist fully within the realm of topsy-turvydom. Disturbing, but objectively ridiculous imagery linked with pleasant emotions, confined to the duration of the dream, but taking on more sinister associated feelings when awake. Usually dreams lose their convincing "antilogic" and power during the day, becoming merely comic. Not so here. Twenty-four hours after this vision of slumber I can rationalise it as ludicrous, but this does nothing to reduce its sinister malevolence.

Maybe I am just a violin, dreaming that I am a violinist!

FRI SEP 12

Nat actually called me "Rod" today, the first time that he has condescended to employ such a familiar mode of address. He is looking very well. He walks about four miles a day now, to and from Greg's house.

And then of course there's the high-energy music that they play. It is not loud, for they seek never to arouse the attention of Greg's family. (Greg's mother never encumbers them, instead leaving trays of vegetarian and vegan food out for the both, for which Nat is most grateful.) However, from what I can ascertain only the wrists and fingers receive the bulk of the exercise, strumming the strings and picking out chords and rudimentary melodies. Nat and Greg egg each other on within their insular world. Like retarded twins, they spend every evening tucked away in Greg's bedroom poring over the history and present forms of their chosen subculture with the intensity of scholars or historians. Why, what is punk but a living fossil? They also swop notes on parasites. Greg is completing a project on this gruesome subject for school, with the emphasis on tapeworms.

Nat's obsession with the macabre doesn't wane. He doesn't spend quite so much time in his unwholesome hidey holes which exist within the extremities of the Snoxell house, but he makes up for it with his perusal of morbid fiction and the study of the lore and facts which lie behind such works. He remains unmoved by Greg's continued harassment of him with things political.

Nat took umbrage when I intimated a thought of mine, that there may be something of a sexual nature betwixt him and his companion. I should have known better. They are quintessentially puritans, however punkoid they perceive their leanings to be.

SUN SEP 21

Nat is being plagued by suicidal thoughts and desires. Some days he will say he is "fine" and refuse to discuss his doom-laden feelings at all. Eventually, however, they return and trouble him to such a degree that he has to share them with me. I still think that he has some "unfinished business". But what to do about it? I cannot tell. I continue to press him to contact me regardless of the hour in which his depression falls, should he feel in danger of taking his life. He feebly agrees to do so but if it came to the crunch, I doubt that he would. Still, one cannot follow someone around for all of their life with a safety net. I suppose I could always give him drugs. . .

I informed Nat of my intention to remain in medicine. He smiled.

MON SEP 22

I had some rather bland dreams last night. The material was so normal and banal that I shan't even bother to record it.

TUE SEP 30

I dropped by at Nat's house today. I caught him just before he set off on his daily excursion to Greg's. He is still receiving his unemployment benefit—just. They send him for interviews, but he doesn't go, so they suspend the giro-cheques for a while and then reconnect him. I passed on to him some information that I have heard, namely that the amount of dole money paid out to individuals is specifically designed to be insufficient to live on. Even with his frugal lifestyle, Nat had detected as much. He dislikes taking the payments, or "benefice-stipend" as he automatically refers to them. He is happiest during the intervals where he receives nothing. However, he is also loath to change his lifestyle. I cannot understand why he refuses to speak to his fellow claimants when he sees them every other week for the "signing on" ritual.

FRI OCT 3

Nat's band have been booked for their second gig, obtained for them through a friend of Greg's mother. It sounds like a highly dubious affair: playing to a hall full of child and juvenile spastics. I hope the hierarchy at the spastics' centre know what they are letting themselves in for. Surely it is imperative for Nat to tone his act down? Perhaps he has already arrived at that decision; after all, a captive audience is guaranteed.

WED OCT 22

Nat's band were pleased with their second live appearance. Jim and Greg had to take a couple of hours off from work and school respectively. The band and their equipment—which although "small" by usual standards was considered plenty big enough for the purpose in hand—were all picked up in a white minibus. As for the concert itself, several children had minor fits and vomitings, one or two defecated on the spot, whilst some even enjoyed it. The majority, however, remained unmoved. The workers at the centre felt it to be a "valuable experience", relieving monotony for patients and staff alike. Still, they would not be requiring the ensemble's services again.

Some of the spastics were very enthusiastic about it all. One demanded the autographs of each member of the band, and Jim's drumsticks. One incident described by Nat was particularly poignant: "one poor fellow with no arms—thalidomide—sidled up to the little stage whilst we were packing up and asked for a kiss. I obliged: on the lips". My guess is that Nat was the more appreciative of this shared intimacy.

THU OCT 30

Nat wants to make a record. He attempted to do such a thing a couple of years ago, but the results had displeased him and he had abandoned the project. This time he is determined to see it through and despite his penchant for being impecunious (or because of it), he has saved just enough money to afford a few hours of recording in a cheap studio. Nat will bear the brunt of the studio fees, or at least Her Majesty's Government will, for Greg spends all of his pocket money on collecting the records other people have put out. Jim considers it an honour for the band to have acquired his services at all, but nevertheless he will be contributing a little cash. Of course I can only go by what Nat tells me, and I think he exaggerates the mercenary tendencies of his partners at times.

SAT NOV 8

Nat's band have been shamelessly exploited by a local recording studio. The tape that they ended up with was nothing like they had envisaged. Nat is more despondent than ever, but only with regard to the band. Curiously, he felt only a "mild twinge" of suicidal despair; his subsequent depression was no more acute than that which anyone else would suffer under similar circumstances. Some setbacks seem to spur him on, whilst others crush him entirely. Fortunately, I think that this disappointment falls into the former category.

MON NOV 24

Nat still fears the dark, but his phobia is now well under control. He no longer feels as if he is going to die when walking past Oval Wood, or going under the bridge at night when returning home from Greg's. He even confessed that, prior to my teaching him fear management, he would often avoid the "scary route" home and make a round trip of some six miles instead. Small wonder he became so healthy looking.

Nat and Greg continue working out new songs and practicing their initial efforts with Jim once a week or fortnight. There is some dissension within the band as to just how well-polished their pieces should become. They do not feel that they are being true to their punk ideals on one hand, but on the other none of them are keen on playing live concerts which, I am given to understand are the natural habitat of the punk band. However, they are not, they claim, a punk band as such, and they are more than a little apprehensive as to what real punks will make of them. Jim thinks that they should just make records and not disappoint the preconceptions of those that purchase those records. Nat and Greg feel that this would be dishonest.

I enquired as to why they couldn't dress up for the evening of a concert. Nat denounced this as the worst possible course of action that they could take. Then I said they should stop staring at their navels and get on with it. Nat's only reply was: "Touché!"

Nat is undoubtedly the controller of the band and its artistic mainspring, but he is also its greatest hindrance.

WED DEC 3

I have noticed that more people are dressed entirely in black. I remarked to Nat that he is in danger of becoming fashionable. Nat does not seem to have a very large wardrobe. Almost everything I have seen him wearing has been black.

SUN DEC 21

Nat does not seem at all worried by the prospect of Christmas, although he does point out that it is "repulsive to celebrate the birth of a peacemaker by devouring the shattered corpse of a festering bird". He also uttered something cryptic about new religions embodying those of ancient times.

1981

SUN JAN 4

Nat spent the festive season in his bedroom doing artwork for his recording project, his family having invited some guests around after last year's more boring celebrations. I asked him about death thoughts, but he said he was okay. I asked him to thank his parents for the big box of biscuits they had sent me—I wasn't so keen on them this time around.

THU JAN 8

I saw Nat's mother in the village. She thought it a good idea that I was gradually "weaning him off". I commented that my pattern of visitations and appointments was not intentional.

SUN JAN 11

I had a dream in which Nat was committed for insanity and his pictures used as toilet paper.

The recurring dream continues. (See sex diary.)

SUN JAN 18

Nat seems quite stable now. When I probe him on his death wish he says "I just don't want to dig into myself". Maybe he has suffered enough, but the prognosis is not good: he might succumb to the first crisis which assails him or, perhaps even worse, avoid anything which he might find stressful (which includes most exciting things) for the rest of his life. He argues, quite logically, that he has achieved a lot within his band. I had to acknowledge this but I also pointed out that the band were making slow and painful progress.

SUN FEB 1

Nat seems quite serious about making a record. He has even obtained copious batches of brochures on the subject. The pressing plants sting the individual or one-off customer quite mercilessly: to get a thousand records with labels in bags, without covers, is going to cost nearly four hundred pounds. Nat will have to borrow this from his slightly begrudging parents. Apparently he is confident that the money can be retrieved by reselling the records, and informed me of a "thriving, if sick, alternative network which specialises in the bizarre and weird". This sounds not unlike the ghettoised world of "classical" records to me.

SUN FEB 22

I wondered if Nat's diet might be a factor contributing to his doom-laden feelings. I got him to write out a list of his weekly intake. Alas, ambivalence prevailed. He must be one of my healthiest patients. He eats much fruit and a lot of raw vegetables. His father grows both on his several allotments, freezing much of the produce for unseasonable consumption. Then there is Nat's own edible fungus harvest. His favourite dish is a foul smelling, but particularly nourishing caudle. All in all, there is no shortage of folic acid, a deficiency in which is currently believed to contribute to depression. Of course, he may be allergic to some of this healthy fodder. He has said that he once overcame an oversensitivity to toadstools via a course of injections. However, he is loath to give up any of it for long enough for me to tell, and I am not sufficiently enamoured of this line of enquiry to pursue it with any great zeal.

SUN MAR 8

Nat seems to be plodding along quite nicely, almost in spite of himself. From a rambling open-ended existence often encapsulating many nocturnal hours, he has evolved a routine, albeit a rather mundane one: signing on one morning every other week; spending the evenings at Greg's; the band's fortnightly rehearsal at Jim's; and his pictures.

TUE MAR 10

I had my most memorable dream of late. It featured Nat, and almost put me off my breakfast.

He liberated an egg from a factory farm, a huge great sprawling mess of a place strewn with effluent, carrying inter alia the fetid corpses of chickens in various states of decomposition. Then Nat scaled a tall red brick wall and rested atop it, with the egg in his lap. The egg expanded from hen size to something an ostrich might produce; it also grew humanesque features like a grotesque humpty dumpty. Nat dropped the egg and it shattered into smithereens, in midair. He jumped after it, somehow managing to re-assemble the mad jigsaw of a monstrosity **in slow motion**, before landing safely on the ground. The ancient-looking egg, successfully put back together again but covered in tiny hairline cracks like a pot stuck back together from shards, then proceeded to bite Nat's head off. **Charming.**

I felt mild-tempered during the dream and the most puzzling aspect, as it was unfurling, was my point of vision. I was continually circling Nat as if I were a satellite of his, completing orbit every few seconds, the rapidity of his movements unable to curtail my curving course.

SUN MAR 29

Nat has been having exceedingly bad luck with the nibs he uses for his miniature drawings, breaking several in the space of only a few weeks. This is not very funny, because he uses only the finest mapping pen tips which are ridiculously expensive. He becomes quite agitated if he has to spend a day without drawing. This does not worry me, for anger seems a positive emotion for Nat. It is only when he begins to reflect on such passionate states that the rot sets in. He has had some death thoughts of late, or at least admitted that such thoughts are often there. Encouragingly, when I enquired where they registered on a scale of one to ten, taking ten as suicide, he was insistent that they rated no more than a four.

SUN APR 19

Today I tried to broach the subject of sex with Nat, but he would have none of it. I don't think I shall raise the matter again, for I detect within him a threat to terminate our Sunday talks over coffee, should I push him too far. That would be a shame as I enjoy his company, but then I enjoy many people's company.

Nat's life is still as insular as ever. When he waffles on about his plans for a record I bring him back down to earth, by making it quite clear that to achieve his admittedly humble ambitions he must first do something **practical**. He then trots out the sordid tale of his last attempt to realise this dream. I remind him that I am willing to administer the occasional push should needs continue to warrant such action.

SUN MAY 3

Nat has arranged for his band to go into a recording studio next month. Both he and Greg have learned well from their previous bitter experience. They have been minutely scouring the covers of their favourite punk records, and have ascertained the most favourable studio from which to acquire the sound they want.

SUN MAY 24

Nat is very excited about the impending recording session. Apparently, the studio is a "squat" in what was once a chic area of South London. It is now terribly dilapidated and avoided by most upright citizens. It sounds like another recipe for disaster to me, but Nat finds it all romantic, in a way only the young can. Aside from this, he has no other news. Tentatively, I probed him about his dreams. He declared that he could not remember any, but he looked somewhat guilty. There are some people so uptight that they cannot have an orgasm even when asleep. I do not think that Nat is quite in this category.

SUN JUN 21

Nat's band recorded the music for their "E.P." yesterday and it all went extremely well. The studio engineer was most helpful "despite being a hippy", and all three members of the band got virtually exactly what they had envisaged. Nat was a little worried about bringing the tape home via the tube train. He had heard that magnetic fields can wipe a tape clean, so the tape was placed in its box then in another box which Nat wrapped in several layers of tin foil. It should be fine if he can ever extricate it from that paper maze. I was so very pleased for him that he had finally achieved a positive experience of the outside world.

They were so engrossed in what they were doing that they did not emerge from the studio for a solid eight hours! The cost of the recording was only half as much as their first abortive attempt, and they got far better results than from that humiliating debacle.

When they did finally crawl out into the twilight, deserted streets littered with bricks and rubble greeted their already vexed countenances. There had been a riot!

Caused by their cacophony, I quipped. Nat was not amused. He pointed out, with childlike logic, that if they hadn't heard the tumult outside the rioters couldn't have heard the music inside either.

SUN JUL 19

Nat has managed to borrow enough money from his parents to get a thousand records pressed and covers printed. The pressing plant, or "depressing plant" as Nat calls it, seems reluctant to complete the work in good time. Nat handed over the majority of the balance in good faith two weeks ago. For fast service, he would have to pay through the nose.

SUN AUG 16

I dropped by at Nat's. He introduced me to Greg, a charming, if reserved young man. He is not at all the "weak freak" of whom Nat had black-humouredly spoken. They were folding up photocopies of Nat's drawings, apparently for record sleeves. I didn't really have a chance to peruse the imagery and miniature hieroglyphics. Nat seemed to be thoroughly enjoying the drudgery; maybe he should have taken a menial factory job after all. They are expecting delivery of the records "any day now". I admire their optimism. This excitement and activity keeps Nat out of mischief.

SUN SEP 13

Nat and Greg finally got the thousand (actually 976) copies of their "E.P.", but not quite as easily as they had foreseen. Somewhat ignominiously, they had to haul them from North London in little brown boxes and black bin liners (how glamorous!) via trains and buses to small shops and independent distribution companies, mostly in the south of the great metropolis, en route housing each disc ad hoc in its prepared photocopied sleeve.

I was exceedingly startled to hear that they have sold them all and have orders for at least the same amount again. One mandarin of the industry, described by Nat as a "perky little imp", even had the perspicacity to foresee a "great future" for Nat within his chosen subgenre. Another company even wanted to press up a further five thousand copies, but Greg is loath to let the record take on its own life and Nat drags along behind him. This may be just as well: I do not like the sound of the scene they are getting into. Nat mentioned something concerning the manager of this record label, "Mouldy Records" or some equally putrid nom de guerre, most of the profits of which go "up his nose". A drug reference from Nat? Surely not. Certainly his lifestyle is not as ascetic as it once was.

The band have made a lot of good contacts—Nat hates this word, I know not why—through their first disc. Indeed Greg has arranged for them to take part in another concert, their third to date. Things really seem to be happening for Nat at long last! Carried along with his enthusiasm, I let him know that I had had some of my writing accepted.

SUN OCT 4

Nat's third gig went well. They were an unknown quantity and had to play first to a cold crowd. So much for anarchy. Not surprisingly the audience differed greatly from those of the band's two previous gigs. It consisted almost entirely of garishly garbed punks. It must be rare for spectators in any arena to be more colourfully clothed than the performers that they have come to see. Consequently cat-calling, cries of "closet cases", and spitting (which I thought was a sign of approval) ensued, but eventually subsided as the gathering grew more accustomed to the music. A few "punters" had even previously bought the record: someone must have I suppose. The ever- resourceful Greg was actually able to sell numerous retained copies after the act had come to an end.

Nat had circulated hundreds of copies of some of his screed, but these were largely ignored and covered the floor like confetti. This, Nat claimed, was probably because "the rabble couldn't read".

"Bitter!" I found myself replying indignantly.

Nearly four hundred people attended the gig: many times the number that frequent my musical soirees. There is, it seems, no accounting for taste. Especially Nat's, for he was repelled by the whole crowd, despite the band's convincing acquittal on their London debut. Greg and Jim "mingled". Nat didn't even try to find kindred spirits. He watched cynically, comparing notes from the "spastic's show" and coming up with many similarities, not least the frenzied attempts at dancing. I suggested it was the band's music that proved to be so consistently emetic. He also mumbled something about "no disparity betwixt intellectual capabilities", although I couldn't tell if he was condemning both peer groups or patronising one more than the other. Still, it is good that he found the playing, in itself, exhilarating. They even got paid for doing it.

WED OCT 14

I dreamt of humble bees and hobbledehoys. I must renounce my occasional indulgence in hashish.

SUN NOV 1

Nat is almost too busy to see me now. He is struggling to get another thousand E.P.s pressed and covers ready. Yet more money has to be begged from the parents! It will be some time before the cheques roll in from the selling of the initial pressing. Ah, the ubiquitous cash flow dilemma! And what do the D.H.S.S. have to say about all this? It seems that Nat will be okay. He is not actively flouting their regulations; indeed, most of the time he is not receiving any "hand-outs" due to his continued nonattendance at job interviews. Nat has become a gentleman of letters. Foolishly, he and Greg put their addresses on the record cover, and now Nat considers it his duty to respond to anyone who has taken the trouble to put pen to paper.

Quite a few cryptic scrawls arrive each day. His favourite correspondent at the moment is one "Puskiss", a fellow artiste of the macabre who lives as far away as America.

He finally gave me a copy of the E.P. today. I was quite touched. Why hadn't he given a locket of his hair free with each one? He blushed.

The sleeve is curious: disappointing drawings compared to those he has shown me; lyrics written out like mediaeval mass. The content, all devised by Nat, is as gothic as anything I had imagined: zombies and curses, sick youths and hearses. There is more wistful and lyrical material too though: rock- pools, towers of strength etc. The label is a "clockwise" foetus that spins dizzily round, 45 revolutions per minute, poor thing.

As to the music itself, I could not suffer a great deal. Most of it is cacophonous. There is a lot of screaming by Nat; a bit scary, but nothing like the primal therapy aberrations, thankfully. Some passages would be unique were it not for a slight fleeting resemblance to the most extreme moments from the canon of that deceased, eccentric English composer Cornelius Cardew. However, it mostly sticks to a rigid and very rapid common-time beat, with Greg and Jim revealed as reasonably competent musicians. Nat just adds volume and bluster with distorted musica in diabola guitar and growling vocals, with the occasional weird whispered overdub: like speaking in tongues, wrought with primitive studio trickery. It is apocalyptic music. This is doubtless why it has had a minor appeal. It is basic, but genuinely eerie.

Nat placed his name at the foot of the small list of credits. (Ah, false modesty.) He once mentioned that there were some "subliminal psychic messages" between the grooves. As a record only has two, long grooves there can only be two such vinyl communiqués. I could not detect anything, but then presumably it would not be subliminal if I could. I am not sure if Nat's mood was jocular or sincere when he put forward this premise. Schumann held similar "invisible writing between the lines" beliefs. Suffice it to say, Nat is not in bad company.

SUN NOV 22

Nat seems to have been galvanised by the work he has to do for the band, and is happy to rattle on at length about the odd correspondent he tends to almost every day. Interest seems sufficiently sustained in the record that even the laxness of the "depressing plant" cannot quench its underground popularity.

Meanwhile, the group arrange new material but, most inexplicably, have no desire to meet their "fans". Nat with "groupies"? Unthinkable!

The death wish lingers, but now plays far less of a role in Nat's life. He is reticent on the matter and I like to think that the good old honest Protestant Work Ethic was all that he needed to banish troublesome emotions and thoughts. After all, isn't this why most people undertake jobs? However, I simply cannot understand anyone who would rather commit their energy and emotions to ink and paper rather than to other human beings.

SUN DEC 13

Not for the first time, Nat has expressed displeasure with his music. At such times he finds solace in drawing and virtually nothing else.

What is he drawing now? Pretty little flowers? Houses?

No, "things". He plans to draw these things nonstop through the festive season.

1982

WAPPING
Autonomy Centre
HATE
B
FOOD
DEATH
HUNGER & PAIN
Evil Evo

SUN JAN 10

Nat took a break from his art commitment to see me today. He quite enjoyed Christmas and was even coaxed by his family into consuming a little alcohol. Why, his severe abstinence stance is crumbling all the while. What next, I ask myself; sex?

I met his mother the other day. She is pleased he has a hobby, but still has hopes of getting him to college. She continually searches out stranger and stranger institutions that might appeal to the youth's oblique sensibilities.

Greg has been taking an active interest in politics, attending weekly assemblies at an "Anarchy Centre", in Wapping of all places. Nat says that its official name is the "Autonomy" centre; a good "Guardian" word. It seems that the band will have to perform there soon. Jim is none too pleased; he would like to take up some of the more lucrative, if as yet tentative offers.

I cannot understand Nat's position in all of this. He seems to want to play the middleman, balancing the extremes. Greg seems to persuade him quite easily and together they overrule Jim. It is all done in the most subtle and subdued of ways. Several passages from the record have been played on the radio. It was a late night programme broadcast nationally, and Nat was surprised that it was obscure to me. It is extraordinary to contemplate that Nat's voice is travelling out into the universe. Indeed, I now feel it an immense relief that he failed to transfer his horrid ululations and ear-splitting squallings from the primal therapy onto tape, vinyl, radio; who knows where else?

SUN JAN 17

Nat's band have been playing numerous gigs at the Anarchy Centre. Greg is most keen on the political aspect. Nat relishes the journey on the underground, under the great river Thames to decayed, ripe-for-renovation Wapping. Actually, you have to go as far as Rotherhithe to pass under Old Father Thames, but I didn't care to disillusion him.

The quaint sight of weirdly garbed faithful wastrels trekking nomadically over the snow to their place of worship pleases Nat immensely. He loves snow, "not as poets and the puerile populace love it, for its great equalising propensities; contrariwise, I find it makes things look vastly different to one another". He was upset at not having seen snowflakes for years and suggested that only children can see such things!

The social side of it he despises: "Macho young men, spikey-haired and leather-clad with their painted punkettes . . . high ideals lost in a haze of alcohol, nicotine, solvents and lysergic acid diethylamide". Nonetheless, many of these "fragmented and demented" souls never fail to appreciate the band's "doomy riffs".

I am sure that most of them will survive the excesses and reckless experiments. Nat cynically tells me that virtually all of the first punk generations—'75', '76, '77—have gone back to "normal" lives, with the one or two notable exceptions being those who managed to exploit the commercial potential of the subculture. Opinion is divided as to whether or not music should address itself to anything other than anarchy, but music cannot be tied down: the harder you try, the more it surprises you with its boundless variety.

"Thud and blunder" is a term applied by certain individuals to the gothic bands such as Nat's. There are other divisions too. Pacifists, and most particularly Greg, are always in danger of being beaten up by those who believe that laws have only ever been changed by violence and not by "wet-arsed liberalism". Ergo, armed revolution will be required to eradicate the constitution entirely, they say.

SUN JAN 31

Nat seems quite keen to see me, to discuss his suddenly abundant news. I am glad he finds life so full and wants to share it with me. Greg has been in contact with some anarchist group which has a large distribution network of its own: records, financing the Anarchy Centre, pamphlets etc. The group has asked the band to record another E.P. for its label. Greg is keen, Nat is wary of such overt politicising, and Jim is upset for he has heard that these people sell their wares virtually at cost price. However, all members of the ensemble are drawn by promises of sales "in excess of ten thousand units". Ah, such is the lure of fame.

SUN FEB 21

Nat has been babbling on incessantly about "characters" who frequent the "A" Centre, as he now calls it. He obtains this erudite biographical data vicariously through Greg, who is becoming something of a social success.

One weird girl, a punk fruitarian, is called "Serpent".

"Her mother was incarcerated in an asylum whilst still a child, for pulling the hair of one of her peers. Several decades later, in 1960 she secretly gave birth to 'Serpent' in an ingle-nook. At first the child was surreptitiously weaned in corridors. On discovery she was adopted as a baby by a vicar, fond of cheap toys and—ironically enough—named Pinchbeck. She never saw her mother again, but her nickname was self-coined and derived from rumours she had heard about her mother's recalcitrance: the poor lady refused to go to the toilet for long stretches at a time. Her sphincter control was so complete that enemas could not be applied and she was invariably pinned to the floor with one nurse pressing down hard on her fat belly. A huge snakelike stool would ooze out, as thick as a wrist. Fortunately, this behaviour and its treatment only came about after Serpent's birth".

Another punk is "Plasticbum". Eccentric names and grotesque life stories seem a prerequisite for assimilation into the "A" Centre. The history of how he acquired this singularly unpleasant sobriquet is far more self-evident than the previous thumbnail sketch. Apparently the poor chap needed much plastic surgery upon his posterior, after simultaneously indulging his twin propensities for meths drinking and lighting up his farts. The most outstanding feature of this fellow, at least as far as Nat is concerned, is that he is "moustachioed". Such facial hair always repulses him except, of course, for that time in the depths of his own despair, when he'd failed to tend to any aspect of his toilet.

Nat has made great efforts to speak to at least one "degenerate", introduced to him by Greg: "The slenderest, palest, and most delicate creature you ever beheld". This "Mark F" is a frail being who eats hardly anything, but Nat assures me that Mark **still feeds from his mother's breast** and has been doing so for the last eighteen years. Such parental dependence is unheard of, but not an impossibility.

Mark lives in Blackly. He is able to regularly travel the fifty odd miles to Wapping, as he is unemployed, and his father works as a guard on the railways so Mark gets privilege tickets.

As a child, the sickly but tenacious Mark F accompanied his father on numerous sojourns along the Blackly to Euston line. On one such outing, Mark F spotted an acephalous corpse upon the tracks. Mr. F stopped the train and, still in shock, ran four hundred yards to the nearest station. He soon returned with a small party of officialdom, only to discover that his son had located the severed skull and was picking at its splattered brains with a stick. Such ghoulish infant curiosity later resurfaced in Mark F's documentation of the incident, a heavily illustrated work of some seventeen volumes, which his father subsequently destroyed.

In adolescence, Mark lost interest in such self-expression. He delved instead into occult lore and now claims to have an English translation of the *Necronomicon*. This, coincidentally, was made under the auspices of the "Black Pope" thus making it immune to later papal censorship, unlike the unauthorised Latin and Greek versions. Much of this work he has committed to memory for fear of what his father would do if he were ever to find it. He now wishes that he could forget what he has learnt, but not even death—or so he says—can save him from his fate. It is not difficult to see why Mark F and Nat should find one another such compelling company.

Nat was glowering as he regaled me with these peculiar tales. I do not think that they were deliberate terminological inexactitudes. Indeed, these stories are not unlike those of the Turin Shroud: more fantastic if they be counterfeit fabrication than if they are the genuine article.

It soon came to light that Nat's slight obstreperousness was due to the fact that he is missing his younger brother, who is now away from home, lodging in a hall of residence whilst studying at the Royal College of Music. The independence and achievement of the junior sibling seem to have slightly undermined Nat's new-found confidence.

SUN MAR 21

Nat's band recorded their second E.P. last weekend. Their "patrons" are committed anarchists, and consequently this record will be different to the band's first effort. Greg has written half of the lyrics. I seem to remember that he only wrote the words to one previous song, something about a tapeworm. Nat's work seems much less original than before. This, however, is exactly what the band want, as opposed to simply reiterating their debut effort, and Nat greatly enjoyed the two days recording. The studio equipment was far more sophisticated than that which the derelict squat had boasted; in fact, it was even graced with state of the art digital technology. Nat took pride in describing it to me. "Yes", I asked him, "but is it punk?"

He blushed. I am glad that the experience seems to have enlivened him.

On the Saturday, the band recorded all of the music and vocals. Nat and Greg eventually got into their sleeping bags well after midnight. Jim went home. Nat got no sleep at all, for the music still pulsated in his head, "fit to explode".

On Sunday they mixed the recordings, settling on a compromise. The band's ideas differed from those of the studio technicians. Nat and Greg got rather pompous about "artistic control", especially considering that they are not even paying a penny towards the enterprise.

The studio people are now talking in terms of "twenty thousand units being shifted", but surely so intensive a workload tends to warp judgement. Jim thinks that the band's lack of image will hold them back, ergo they should cease to appear live and become even more of an enigma. Greg demands that they play more gigs and Nat follows suit, probably out of boredom. Nat says the studio is not known for the prompt release of its products: a conservative estimate is the end of Summer.

WED MAR 31

Witnessed a birth today. I thought of Nat. Forceps were greatly utilised.

SUN APR 11

Nat has been seeing a lot of his new friend Mark F. Indeed, he has even discovered what the mysterious F stands for. Curiosity got the better of him, so he plucked the entire F section for the town of Blackly from a phone box directory and perused it at his leisure whilst sitting, gently gyrating, upon a roundabout in a deserted children's playground. As fortune would have it, he soon found a name to match Mark's address: Farinelli. Superfluous to say, Nat then pasted the entire section of Blackly names beginning with "F" back in the temporarily vandalised telephone directory. The world's most famous singer, an eighteenth-century virtuoso castrato, also went by this name.This fact led almost inevitably to the teasing and bullying of Mark at school, hence his reluctance to carry the family name into adult life.

Mark was a little upset with Nat at first for prying into his "skeleton in the cupboard". However, on hearing of Nat's own metaphorical and indeed literal embodiment of that hackneyed phrase, he confessed to a great pride in his Italian pseudoaristocratic surname. Mark did stress that Nat was not to pass on this newly gleaned fragment of highly personal information. It is pleasing that Nat knows that he can trust me. Mark Farinelli also has a band and the two have been sharing gigs, mainly in deconsecrated churches, and very successfully.

Nat and Mark also share an abhorrence of the telephone, to the degree that they wish that Mr. A.G. Bell had been drowned at birth! Ironic, then, that it was via the accoutrements of this device that Nat came to know Mark's name.

Nat's phobia of telephones dates back to a bad childhood experience when he picked up the receiver, only to be frightened by a "disembodied doomy voice" booming at him. However, the postal service suits their purposes quite nicely. It is they who insist on terrorising innocent G.P.O. employees. Only the other week Nat sent Mark a minute papier mache coffin, with scarcely enough room for stamp and address, and with a plasticine "baby" inside. The words, scrawled in a tiny hand, were: "to be received by Marco Farinelli . . . if undelivered please bury". Incredibly, it did arrive at the Farinelli household, completely crushed but much to "Marco's" delight. Nat now awaits with bated breath to see what abomination Mark can concoct by way of a reply.

I suggested that they curtail these excesses lest they infringe obscenity laws. Nat casually informed me that Mark's epistolary endeavours had already engendered a visit from the "Blasphemy Squad"—I have never heard of such an entity before. Certain indecent comments had been written about Jesus Christ on an envelope. Mark was let off with a stern warning, but he was not sufficiently shaken to cease embellishing his missives entirely.

SAT MAY 1

My dreams seem interminably dull of late, with the exception of one which woke me up last night. I dreamt, or rather "nightmared", that Nat's head fell gently apart into shards so small as to be invisible. Each shard landed upon a star. The anterior part of his body did not so much explode as travel innumerable light years in seconds.

SAT MAY 9

Nat and Mark have so much in common. They are virtually the same age and both dolefully on the dole. Also, they are both obsessed by things morbid. I am sure that they cannot be good for one another.

Nat sees less of the increasingly political Greg and more of the macabre Mark. At one time they were going to manufacture—in large quantities—Nat's eldritch art object, the horrid dead baby in a coffin, but thankfully the practicalities of such a dubious venture deterred them. Mark still frequents the "A Centre", but Nat doesn't go unless Greg has got the band a gig there.

Nat certainly leads a less sequestered life than when I first encountered him, but I'm not sure if it's enough. Occasionally he admits that the death wish, though it may not be so obvious now, still "lurks in the wings".

SUN MAY 30

Nat's friends, Greg and Mark, have been tarrying in London after gigs, sampling the squatters' lifestyle. Nat is very dismissive of their experiments, probably jealous of their growing thirst for independence. The drummer in Nat's band, Jim, has also moved away from home recently, and I have gained the impression that Nat is being gently mocked of late as a mother's boy.

This image is not entirely a true one. Even during his phase of acute clinical depression he tended to his own needs, the practical ones at least, far better than many men manage in a lifetime. However, he is not keen to sever the symbolic umbilical cord. He never gets into "real" arguments with his parents, unlike Greg and Mark. Mark's father recently cut off an overelaborate "hair fetish" from his son's already extravagant coiffure. The deepest emotions are invariably expressed through superficial appearances at this stage. I see a lot of cases like this.

SUN JUL 4

Nat's band's first E.P. is doing very well in America. The studio has recently taken over its pressing and distribution, somehow making it possible to earn the band more money whilst selling the individual records at almost cost price. Apparently, over there such music is known as "hardcore", which sounds rather rude to me. Nat has paid back the cash that he borrowed from his parents. In Europe and America they have sold five thousand records; Nat says that they are a "cult band within a subculture". I don't imagine for one moment that they will ever make a living out of it, but the knowledge Nat is gaining must be useful, if only as an ego-booster.

SUN JUL 25

Nat's band's second E.P. was released last week. He says it was reviewed in one of the music papers, where it was labelled "demoniac". It has already sold more than the first E.P., but this is not representative, as Nat informs me that X number of people automatically purchase whatever the anarchist studio puts out. Nat seemed a little disappointed that the studio only pressed ten thousand copies. Such caution is understandable, however, as the band are reluctant to promote their work in any way. They do have one or two gigs in London on the horizon, with Mark's band as usual, but this is purely co-incidental.

Meanwhile Mark and Greg have been brow-beating Nat, trying to get him to spend a night in a squat. He is loath to do this and even regrets the night he was away from his bed whilst recording the second E.P. His oddity of a house scares him and yet he loves it so. He admitted that, prior to the recording session, the last time he had been away from the house for any length of time was over ten years ago. His older brother had refused to join in the family holidays, and Nat had stayed at home with him. I made it abundantly clear that any break from the intense environment of his house might not go amiss, even if it were only for one night spent curled up on a flea-ridden mattress in a filthy squat in London town.

FRI AUG 27

I dropped by at Nat's today. He gave me a copy of his latest waxing. It is a lot less idiosyncratic than the first offering, consisting largely of regurgitated pseudopolitical rantings from Greg, profusely and turgidly illustrated on the cover with half-hearted scratches by Nat. Overall, it is far less morbid and more of a satirical work: an update on some of Dean Swift's pamphlets, with just a twinge of the macabre. The band are becoming smug and self-satisfied, but I don't like to disturb this false sense of security if it makes Nat happy. He certainly believes that to achieve even limited popularity one has to embrace banality with total abandon. Such hard-boiled realism seems so far removed from his attitude of only a year ago. I sense that he perceives my realisation of this. Nat likes to see me but confides in me less. He is becoming strong. I confess it makes me a little sad in a perverse sort of way.

SUN SEP 26

Nat is very worried about his friend Greg, who seems to be in constant pain. "Physical, spiritual or existential?" I asked.

I instantly regretted my flippant remark as Nat described Greg's condition: he has been receiving medication for a swollen testicle, probably orchitis—most likely a psychosomatic illness brought on by the dichotomy of being in an "anarchist band" whilst continuing studies in the sixth form of one of the "system's" comprehensive schools. His obsessive studies of the effects of parasites on the human body might account for the nature of the illness.

SUN OCT 31

Nat seems to have returned to living vicariously. He speaks incessantly of the dramatic events that are shaping Greg's life. His friend has left school. He also can no longer tolerate the hypocrisy of living with his parents and now resides at several addresses, the majority of which are squats.

As if this were not enough, his testicle has been surgically removed and his illness diagnosed as cancer. Of course, I have no knowledge of the case but metastases are likely. Their early treatment will probably be successful, especially for one so young. However, I did not let on to Nat that the medical profession remains puzzled by much of the newly gleaned information about cancer. I did say that the latest therapies are very effective and Nat looked suitably impressed, so I didn't mention that we don't know how they work exactly. Greg has been studying the disease, obsessively scrutinising any book he can lay his hands on. Some of the other books in his reading list don't sound such a good idea: Nat mentioned the diary of Bobby Sands. Indeed Nat is a little squeamish about the whole affair, but he has been visiting Greg regularly in hospital, despite his abhorrence of such places—he still faints at the sight of blood. Mark cannot cope with the idea of visiting Greg at all. Happily though, many of Greg's squatter friends keep a vigil at his bedside, much to my colleagues' annoyance, no doubt.

Nat was keen to speculate on the more abstract implications of Greg's malady. He compared his own life closely with that of Greg's—which he now knows intimately—making out a case for the genuine existence of the much-touted "cancer personality". He also uttered a long diatribe against any possibility of a "suicide personality", but was unable to separate himself from his own experience here.

Nat has constantly tried to get Greg to vary his staple diet of bread, cheese, chocolate and little else, but failed. Eventually he got so wound up that he could do no better than quote "**life** is the disease".

SUN NOV 28

The prognosis for Greg is good. Although he has secondary deposits on his chest they are only minor, and he has been undergoing chemotherapy.

Greg has broken all ties with his family and refuses to see them. I continually registered my concern with Nat that sleeping on park benches, or indeed in squats, between treatments is not conducive to complete recovery. Nat fully agrees with me and, much to Greg's dismay, he still sees Greg's distraught parents, who firmly believe that their son's "anarcho cronies" are "signing his death warrant". As he did with the band, Nat has set himself up as a type of middleman, not fully trusted by either side, but the only person with access to both parties.

Greg is convinced that it was his parents' attitude which elicited his illness in the first place. This sudden, devastating unleashing of anger is very common and understandable with life-threatening illnesses. It is a particularly ubiquitous occurrence with "the big C".

Nat simply cannot fulfil the self-appointed dual role of consoling Greg's family whilst remaining loyal to his friend. He seeks advice but I cannot offer any. And what of his life outside these embroilments? Nothing.

SUN DEC 19

Nat's band have been rehearsing music for an album, under Greg's brave insistence. Fortunately, the new material is a lot slower than usual, but Greg still needs a great deal of rest between songs. Gigs, of course, are out of the question, which is a little sad as the band have been offered some choice concerts of late. Nat believes this to be out of a morbid interest in Greg's condition which, many rumours would have it, is **dead**. It is Greg who is the most alarmed by his own appearance. Many people cope admirably with the side-effects of chemotherapy; hair falling out etc. Greg, however, seems to find them more distressing than the disease itself.

Leichenwagen

1983

SUN JAN 23

Greg has been in and out of hospital, conforming rigidly to the regime of chemotherapy. He was glad he did not have to spend Christmas on the ward. Nat speaks of Greg's life as if it were his own. One has to pry with unremitting fortitude in order to unravel the barest glimpses of his own daily routine. Nat is doing artwork for the proposed album, which he says the anarchist studio will be releasing. I am not so confident since reading about the studio's latest offering in *The Times*: apparently it was a vicious condemnation of the government's handling of the Falklands crisis. Questions pertaining to the "obscene phonographic recording" were raised in the House. Who will issue Nat's records if the anarchist studio gets taken to the cleaners, I wonder? Philips? It was good to see Nat laugh.

After a long silence on the subject, Nat was finally coaxed into speaking about his death wish. He wouldn't mind dying, but he does not actively seek oblivion. It is impossible to tell how great an impact Greg's disease has made on Nat. I gave Nat a lift home. He put his seat belt on, something he only started to do after it was made illegal not to wear one. It seems Nat is prepared for death but not for arrest.

SUN FEB 13

I find it alarming that Nat's taste for the macabre shows no sign of waning, despite the plight of his friend Greg. He wants their album to have the word "death" in the title. He would also, it seems, be quite prepared to talk of the things he has seen on the cancer ward for hours, as if even I were someone totally unfamiliar with such material. He does, however, have a compelling way of conveying his reactions: after all, this is his first actual contact with death. He spoke at length about one young man in the ward, who was older than Greg but much younger than most of the other patients, and who "coughed something up which melted the floor". The staff permitted him to eat whatever he desired. Consequently his diet consisted almost entirely of "coconut creams".

Nat was shocked that this young man was left to die.

"Perhaps he wanted to die", I intervened, interrupting Nat's train of thought. He was clearly stumped. Nat had previously overlooked the possibility of another person's death wish. "Yes, it takes many forms",

I added. Nat then went off on a tangent. Try as I might I could not curb his vociferousness.

I fear that the boy is relapsing once more. He seldom goes out save for visiting Greg, which he does less and less, and for the occasional band practice. Even signing on is done on a monthly basis now, due to the swelling of the ranks of the unemployed. Mark has avoided direct communication with Nat and Greg. I assured Nat that disease often scares people away, but he takes such affronts so very personally. His correspondence is blossoming to many letters a day, but what use are "paper dreams"? Still, I am here if he needs me.

MON FEB 21

I dreamt I could hear heavy breathing emanating from within my skull. The phrase "whirlpool of tears" entered my head. One is forcibly reminded of the alcohol-induced reveries of Poe. Henceforth I shall not bother to record or even recollect my nocturnal visions. Dreams are unimportant.

SUN MAR 20

Greg's anger at his illness, having long since exiled his parents, has now turned on Nat. Greg's anarchist friends have been urging him to seek a homeopathic remedy for his disease. Although Nat is cynical about modern medicine, frequently disparaging the testing of drugs upon innocent animals—a procedure he claims is refuted by the phenomenon of thalidomide—under my influence he entreats Greg to continue with the chemotherapy. Greg sees this advice as symptomatic of Nat's own overreliance on the medical profession—me!—and scorns him for it. Indeed, Greg is increasingly shaping his life according to his strict code of ethics, refusing even to take the state's money. Hence Nat's lifestyle comes in for much derision. Greg's illness has cured him of one thing: his love of the macabre.

The band is still holding together, but only just. In Greg's eyes Nat is an outcast and Jim is a leper. Yet although the music they play together would be sufficient to purge most souls for a lifetime, it does not seem to assuage Greg's anger in the slightest. Under such circumstances, Nat's pessimistic theories as to the ineptitude of catharsis would seem most plausible, were it not for the fact that Greg's chemotherapy is in itself a purgative treatment which leads him to a more personal, less artistic but nevertheless more genuine catharsis than anything Nat has envisaged for himself.

SUN MAR 27

Nat's band were due to record their album today, but Greg cancelled the session at the last minute. This was not directly due to his illness, but rather a gesture to show Jim and Nat just how bad he feels. Nat's main interest lies with the record and not where it should which is with his friend. I greatly berated him for this.

It was soon apparent why Nat had arranged our sudden appointment. He is in a state of confusion himself, having been up all night embellishing and finishing off artwork for the project. The nub of the problem seems to be the acute difference betwixt Greg and Nat's lifestyles. Greg feels that the way of life he has chosen should also be adopted by Nat. This, telling people what to do, does not in itself seem very anarchistic. Nat believes that it is "the illness that speaks".

By the end of our meeting Nat had drunk vast quantities of coffee, a habit for which Greg condemns him, because the space in the third world used to grow such "luxurious indulgences" could be better used for growing crops to feed the starving who live there. Nat has gradually resigned himself to never seeing Greg again and the album never coming to fruition. I suggested there was an element of cherchez la femme on Greg's side; Nat would neither confirm nor deny this suspicion of mine.

SUN APR 10

Nat's band finally recorded their album.

In the end Greg did it—"for the money". At least that is what he says.

Nat told me the three days spent recording and mixing were unexpectedly pleasant. Just getting on with the task, as it were. Greg undertook this strenuous task with the blessings of his doctors, who probably sought to appease their patient in view of his misguided inclinations to take his custom elsewhere. They do not know what to make of Greg's stringent use of the latest "imaging" and "visualisation" techniques for combating cancer imported from America. Such dabbling cannot be harmful, and belief in such vagaries may even have a placebo effect. I must swot up on these new phenomena.

The people from the studio were none too pleased or sympathetic with Greg for messing up the first recording session, at one point even suggesting a replacement bassist. Happily, Nat and Jim are not that cruel. Nor were the studio pleased with the music at first, until Jim, of all people, convinced them of its viability. The studio also had to ferry the three nonmusicians home each night to their respective abodes, which also

irked. Finally it was Nat's artwork and fiendish growling and wailing vocal extemporisations that saved the day.

Nat has seen his old friend Simeon recently. Simeon had a bad cold. "What's this effect you have on people?" I queried. He chortled and glowered most theatrically. He must be missing his live appearances.

I shall not be able to see Nat for a while because of various extra commitments—army medicals etc.—and my week off hang-gliding.

SUN MAY 22

Nat's friend Greg died on April 30th: Nat's birthday.

Nat is left with a complicated array of emotions. The two friends had already parted acrimoniously, the last time they met being at the recording studio almost a month before. Nat does not seem too upset: he hasn't wept at all, but then grief takes many forms.

I questioned him in great detail about the death. It was nothing like I had imagined. Greg had continued with the chemotherapy. He hadn't opted for alternative medicine, which was the scenario I had pictured. Nat's image of Greg, which he had passed on to me, was one of recovery. So rapid and **unexpected** a demise is always shocking, even when relayed second-hand and after much experience of death. Greg's doctors remain baffled. Cobalt lymph node tests, body scans and the like revealed no further spread of cancer seedlings. The areas affected were not critical: primarily the chest but also, to a much lesser extent, the stomach. Even these tumours were thought to be under control. There was no residual cancer in the remaining testicle.

Nat described the postmortem in some detail: "when they opened him up, huge tracts of his body were riddled with cancer. They wanted to find out why all their probing and dissecting, with the zeal of vivisectionists, had not even hinted as much, but Greg's parents would not consent to more tests".

Apparently, the coroner was old Blinkensop, which is a shame because I do not know him well enough to learn more of the matter. Greg's parents, who have a family plot at the cemetery, arranged their son's funeral but did not attend. This is a decision that I fear they will come to bitterly regret. They did inform Nat of the burial ceremony and he in turn passed on the information to Greg's anarchist friends, none of whom chose to honour the obsequies. Nat was the only mourner.

Nat has coped well with the conflicting emotions. He inevitably harbours a certain amount of guilt for what happened to Greg, although not as excessively as one might expect from such an anxiety addict. Indeed, he has done very well to survive the initial stages of such a trauma.

It **was** Nat who clogged my telephone answering machine full of blank messages. This is understandable in the event, but I wish he could come to terms with telecommunications.

WED MAY 25

I dropped by at Nat's house today. He rather resented my "checking up" on him. He seemed well balanced, as if he'd somehow worked through much of his grief prior to Greg's death. I advised him not to lose contact with Jim and the people at the studio. A glow of perversity illuminated his dull eyes.

SUN JUN 26

The studio has already released Nat's band's debut and swansong album. Nat brought me a copy today, his only one, which he insisted I must keep.

The whole thing reeks of **death**. It is not so much a requiem, as something specifically wrought to be **posthumous**: like a suicide note. The music is unremittingly melancholic; even Nat's gruff voice lacks venom, and his screams are instead fairly ethereal. Their previous efforts jumped in and out of major and minor modes, whereas the album is all in minor keys, with diminished sevenths inexplicably creeping in. Not surprisingly, the late Greg's bass playing lacks the lyricism and frenzied flourishes of the two E.P.s. Jim's drumming is confined almost entirely to boomy, thunderous thuds. The words to the songs are poetical as ever. The overall effect is still abrasive and it's difficult for one of refined sensibilities to endure prolonged exposure. Intuitively one gains the impression that it is not contrived. **They didn't know what they were doing**.

The studio has pressed ten thousand copies of which seven thousand have already been "shifted". This is a modest amount according to Nat, who has seen the sales sheets of more garishly garbed, self-promoting, fashionable bands on the studio's books. The studio have got a damned nerve putting the product out without even consulting Greg's parents. They will of course get Greg's royalties from the disc, but if I were them I might be inclined to sue.

I asked Nat why he thought he had managed to survive the upheaval of recent weeks, without being inundated with death thoughts. He mumbled some allusion to the suicide rate dropping off at times of war. It is true he has been so steeped in death of late, one way or another, that he may even be living disproof of his own anticatharsis ideas. I believe purgation is possible, but not within the restricted parameters of today's society.

Nat is disenchanted with the record; his insistence that I should have his only copy makes this quite clear.

I told him he should feel very proud of the cover artwork. It depicts a miniscule filigree of cretinous creatures, headless popes, demoniac archangels, angelic demoniacals, necrophiliac nuns etc. etc. Many heads are severed or seem to exist independently of bodies; each one is depicted screaming. The screams are not those of the twentieth century so familiarised by Munch and Bacon, but instead they hark back down the generations to primaeval times in a far more convincing manner. There is also a huge poster, which against Nat's wishes is a blow-up of the original drawing. It still, however, requires detailed study before offering up the many weird objects that lurk within its withered maze of twisted, labyrinthine, nightmarish weeds. Such astounding anfractuosities! Nat refused to be cajoled into discussing his macabre masterwork. However, he did accept my compliments most gracefully.

SUN JUL 31

Nat has become reclusive once more. I do not feel that I can push him, for he is still grieving for Greg and working through his feelings of guilt. He has cut down tremendously on his epistolary activities too, retaining just one or two cherished correspondents. Where once the sheer universality of youth disaffection enlivened him, it now serves only to sadden the poor boy. This is not a mellowing of character on Nat's part: indeed, he sees the whole rebellion phenomenon as just another phase on the path to death, "like learning bowel control".

Was he missing gigging? Apparently not. He says he had felt like a circus freak with his band, exhibiting his odd life history and Greg's deformity and demise to a mocking, leering, spiteful audience; casting pearls to swine. I assured him that this was not how he perceived events at the time, and that it is his present state that is colouring his memory. I offered my opinion that future retrospections, I am sure, will allow Nat to view those times with correct perspective and fond recall. He was duly touched.

SUN SEP 4

Nat stays in much more than I would like. His visits to me make up the bulk of his outings, and even his monthly signing-on trips to the Labour Exchange have been terminated. The D.H.S.S.—or S.S. as Nat calls them—

gave him a harrowing interview, with regard to his extracurricular musical activities. "Kafka's not the only one" I said, glad I had got to use this line at last. He could not answer their accusations, and when they asked for proof of his attendance at job interviews, he had none.

They said he had been going on like this for aeons and where would it end? Would they eventually have to wheel in his file on a trolley?

"So what?" I said, and Nat cheered up. They can only stop his money if he deliberately misleads them about record royalties or fails to attend their appointments. However, he is loath to engage with them at all, ergo he has been forfeiting his entitlements. He would rather eke out an existence on the music money than go begging to "those people".

I tried to reason with him, explaining that the system was not intended to cope with such large numbers and how that places an unbearable strain on D.H.S.S. staff, but he would have none of it. He has told them that he does not require their charity any longer. In a fit of pique the Unemployment Resettlement Officer directed him to class himself as permanently unemployable, which has done nothing for his self-image. The money from the record, whilst doubtless a fair share of the humble profits, is hardly enough to live on. However, Nat has returned once more to his ascetic existence and is happy if he merely has sufficient cash to pay his parents his keep each week.

It is strange, but I have never really known him free from suicidal tendencies or out of mourning. The most difficult part of his grieving is over. Nat has achieved a truly disinterested way of life. His family almost ignores him; even his mother no longer expects much of him. The pattern of family life has adapted to Nat's protracted behaviour. Any ruffling of the atrophic structure has to be quickly subdued.

In days gone by, Nat would have been chained into one of his secret chambers. Instead, he himself chooses to linger in those sickly cubby-holes unbeknown to parents and siblings. The end result is much the same. Nat's twin penchants for weird vegan food and long hours spent over a drawing board remain unimpinged. Were this not so I fear I might be forced to section the boy; not for his sake, but for mine.

SUN DEC 4

I confess that I have been leaving Nat to his own devices of late, due to a combination of overfamiliarisation with the facts of his case, and the continual return to a state of impasse. None the less, this didn't prevent me from enjoying his company today.

We took coffee in my study. He looked almost lively after his rare airing, and I recommended more regular imbibings of atmospheres other than the charnel house variety. He muttered some allusion to expanding one's lungs with carbon monoxide; we were both amused.

Nat has long since ceased to take "doctor's orders" seriously. Perhaps I should issue a contrariwise diagnosis in order to set him on the right path. I fear that this would also fail. Nat would be only too pleased were I to fall under the same imp of the perverse as he.

Certainly one could never imagine Nat seeking a second opinion. I am sure he comes to see me as a person and not as a psychologist. Maybe he would be less immune to my charms if I were to wear a white coat and insist on seeing him only at the surgery.

I asked him if he had been anywhere, done anything, seen anyone?

He went quiet and looked very thoughtful before saying he had seen Simeon.

When?

Four months ago. His life is taking on a timescale normally only associated with the eighties and over. I suggested he was not ready for his pipe and slippers just yet.

1984

FRI JAN 6

I was sad not to receive my usual festive gift of a box of biscuits from the Snoxells this year.

SUN FEB 26

It's now about four years since I first met Nat. He leads the most sequestered existence of anyone I have ever known. I am now so familiar with his personality that I believe he leads such a life half out of a genuine proclivity, and half out of fear of what is unfamiliar to him. I still like to think he will venture into the outside world when he is ready. I urge him to do so but I cannot force him.

He tells me that the accumulated royalties from his records are running out. Not before time either. Even he cannot stretch the pennies that far.

His left eye was very bloodshot and he summoned up the courage to ask me why. It was obvious: it is the eye over which his fringe hangs. He is allergic to his own hair. I have noticed that when it is long, he has a most appealing way of flicking his head back so as to banish any offending tresses from his face. It is a most singular action.

FRI APR 27

Nat is still strenuously avoiding gainful employment, but manages to give sufficient money to his parents to appease them. He looks incredibly unwholesome. It is, however, difficult to gauge his actual state of health, as his appearance has always been weird. His hair is very long and lank and now clings to his neck. This is made even more bizarre by his solution to the bloodshot eye problem: he has cut off his fringe entirely. This quaint coiffure is as singular as the house in which he lives.

I told Nat about the many successes I have had using primal therapy on a large number of "patients", most of them friends. He was greatly shaken, as if he had imagined himself to be my one and only "baby". He soon recovered his equilibrium when I revealed that I have yet to witness a more violent reaction than that which his regression sessions had produced. He even gesticulated in a mildly frenzied manner with his spindly, agile and twig-like, lily-white fingers. This prompted me to enquire about his weight.

"Thinnest live longest" came the improvised rhyme of a reply. This unexpected outburst of optimism could hardly be met with agreement.

WED JUN 20

I am glad to know that Nat is keeping up with his correspondence. Any outside contact, however second-hand, is to be encouraged. He hasn't seen Simeon (who married a wealthy antipodean lady) for ages. He showed me a letter from his friend and old Anarchy Centre cohort Mark, with whom he has recently reestablished contact; strictly on an epistolary basis, of course. The missive was impregnated with a sickly smell which seemed already known to me, and yet whose origin I didn't care to elicit. It went on at great length about "the old days at Wapping". I got the impression that Mark's life is not immensely dissimilar to Nat's. They put into letters what most people discharge daily into conversation. Mark seems, of the two, the more eccentric. If I deciphered his noxious scrawl correctly, he is unable to sleep in his bedroom at night, having painted it in his favourite colour, black. He has not found the result conducive to slumber, for he fears he might take his rest during the daylight hours. It is now his plan to paint the room white and sleep **all** day.

However, Nat contradicted my assumption, confiding in me that he and Mark share certain feelings of doom, but that Mark has never seriously contemplated suicide, and cannot fully relate to Nat's darkest emotions. Was Nat boasting or complaining? A little of both, I imagine. I suggested that he needs an alternative to Mark. He disagreed.

WED AUG 15

When I went to see Nat today, he complained of noises in his left ear. I could not examine him because I didn't have my black bag with me. He described the sounds as comparable to a thousand screaming serpents slithering in a sea of wax and slime. I have heard tinnitus described in many ways, but never as exotically as this.

I suggested treatment but he refused, claiming that the ear fault made him occasionally angry but not depressed and that he could "handle it". Anyhow, he had read in a copy of "Harpers & Queen" (of all things) that little can be done about the complaint. He enjoys the aloofness from the world which it gives him.

He looks so very pale. I suggested that anaemia might be the cause of this, but he continually refused my offers to return him to a specialist. Actually, anaemia is a very rare cause of tinnitus. It is, however, the only thing I can think of, given that Nat strenuously denies having subjected himself to any loud noise. This complaint is usually only associated with trigger happy, aged farmers. I told Nat he was old before his time. He seemed to treasure this flippancy, if indeed it was flippancy.

Nat blurted out something about Mark being a "missing person". He fears his friend will fare badly without his mother's milk. I could not discern if this was an example of his warped humour or if he was telling the truth: his fictitious constructions and effusions are so elaborate that only he now holds the key to them. His ability to tell reality from fantasy has advanced to such a degree that I regard him as one of the sanest people I know.

TUE NOV 13

Nat seems to have lost all interest in anything, describing his mood as "ultra-atrabilious". He has totally relapsed into his old nocturnal habits. I am convinced that this is an affectation: it does not follow the sleep pattern ingrained in his childhood and I am inclined to favour the populist attitude that people who prefer to be awake at night do so only because they do not like what goes on during the day.

Nat attempted to refute this, saying that he would sleep the whole day if he could, but this simply confirms my feeling that his only desire is for oblivion. In some ways, Nat has reached his lowest ebb in all the time I have known him. He has completely abandoned writing long letters and drawing, the things that used to give him pleasure. Even his previous unflappable obsession with eating healthily has diminished to the point that he looks almost anorexic. His room was littered with empty ice cream cartons of every conceivable flavour, and the sell-by dates had long since expired. His vegan principles must have collapsed before his appetite: nowadays ice "cream" contains no dairy products, but pigs' blood is widely used in its manufacture. I fear his body must have reacted violently to the sudden influx of animal-based products, perhaps accounting for the ensuing aversion to food.

I cannot imagine that he would desire, even subconsciously, to be back in his mother's womb, given his intimate knowledge and memory of that traumatic era as supplied to him by primal therapy.

I cannot help thinking I have failed him. I have always wondered if he held the seldom encountered but well-documented view that his entire life was a mistake and that he should never have been born at all. There are individuals cursed with this harrowing affliction, and premature death is almost inevitable in such cases. Nat has always protested most strongly that he is not among their number, but I now have reason to doubt him. Nat's self-hatred is matched only by the callous indifference of his family. They have continually ignored my admonitions with regard to their second son. They have even threatened me with legal action should I persist in seeing Nat.

It is as if Nat has some contagious, character-blighting disease which has spread throughout his family. I have certainly misjudged the Snoxells. My mind is full of the wildest speculations. Perhaps they are a paranoid family after all, carrying out their own cathartic experiment with Nat as the human sacrifice.

It's been hinted at by my friends and colleagues that I am rationalising my failure. Friends! It's not as if I've ever had a case suicide on me. This is something very different. My "friends" suggest that the family's reaction is not unreasonable, seeing as how the subject has unremittingly drenched them all in his own death wish for so long. I am under no ethical obligation and should really just wash my hands of the whole affair, but I am captivated, or rather, infatuated by . . . **something**. Desperate as Nat's situation is, it is not sufficiently acute to have him sectioned. Ideally, the whole family should be incarcerated.

1985

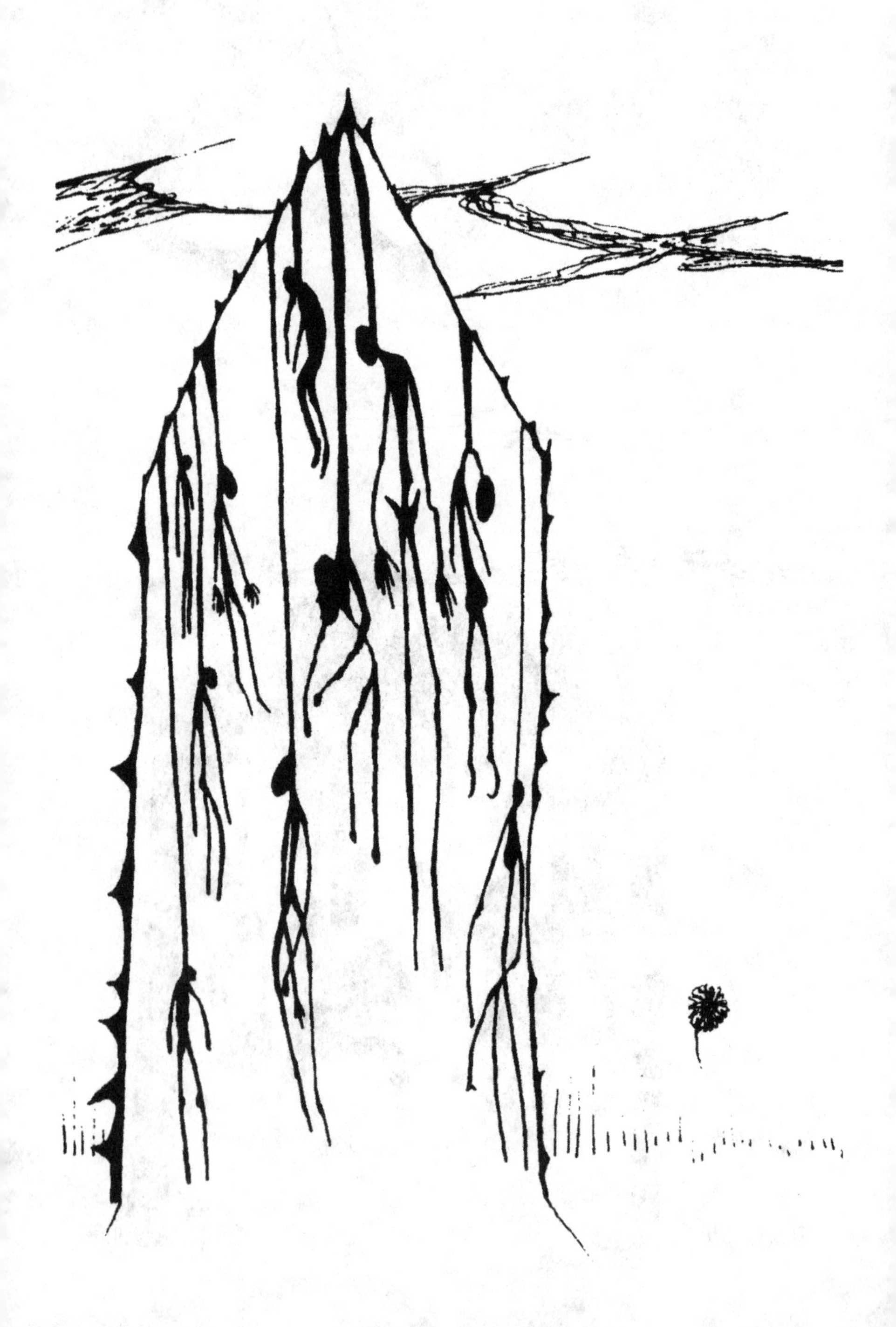

SAT FEB 9

I have taken friends' advice and put Nat out of my mind. It is not easy. It requires much meditation.

SUN MAY 5

Anarchists desecrated the grave of Greg, once a friend of Nat's, on the anniversary of his interment. There was a hysterical botch of a report in a local paper. Thankfully the corpse was not purloined as intended, for the would-be body snatchers were disturbed before even reaching the casket. The tombstone was daubed with obscene graffiti and as yet unidentified symbols.

MON JUL 9

Whilst out walking with friends in the twilight, we had to go under a railway bridge; I thought of Nat. I do hope he is okay. I have heard nothing of the Snoxell family for ages.

WED SEP 4

I was very sad to hear of the death of Mr. Thistle, the local historian and anthropologist. It was not totally unexpected; he was after all a nonagenarian, although he seemed blissfully unaware of the fact. I wish I had met him more than once.

TUE SEP 24

I attended the funeral of Mr. Thistle, which has been much delayed due to wrangles over his death-bed plea to be buried in Black Langley churchyard, an honour granted only to the village's most illustrious inhabitants, since plots unaffected by water-table subsidence have for centuries been few and far between. In the end it was the vicar, really a most neurotic fellow, who insisted out of some irrational fear for the vicarage chimney pots that Mr. Thistle's last wish be granted. There were many mourners; mostly strange, wizened old folk whom I have never seen before.

On returning home, I read the pamphlet Mr. Thistle had given me five years ago. The stories about Nicholas Blackspear, the infamous "Black Pope" who "gave" Ireland to Henry II, and the atrocities he perpetrated are gruesomely entertaining, though as the footnotes acknowledged, almost entirely apocryphal.

WED NOV 20

I saw Nat in the village today. At least, I **think** it was him.

A gaunt, haggard figure leapt out from the butcher's shop, spreading a trail of sawdust-confetti in its wake. Thick black hair covered the monstrosity's face, as if to hide it. Then the thing flicked its head, jettisoning the hair from its face in a manner singularly reminiscent of Nat. It carried a dead piglet runt under its arm. Then, most alarmingly, it wrenched the unplucked corpse of a game bird from a rack on a door and bit its head off in one go, revealing viridescent peg-like teeth, several of which had been sharpened into evil-looking spikes.

By this time a small crowd had gathered to show their outrage at this disgusting behaviour. The creature's hypersensitive, bloodshot eyes perceived my form. The necrophiliac geek turned and bolted down the street.

The butcher appeared, a huge carving knife in his hand, looking equally as intent on violence as Nat had. I calmed him down and paid for the stolen goods. The crowd gradually dispersed. If that **was** Nat, he has regressed to some appalling subhuman, bestial state.

This evening I telephoned the Snoxell home. The message was garbled and I could not identify the speaker, but it seems that Nat has not been seen for a year.

I said that I had had a sighting of him in the village today. There was no reply. I shouted, but heard only sinister, echoing laughter. I tried redialling, but to no avail. Something must be done, but what? I cannot tell. I feel so drained.

THU NOV 21

Dear diary,

As I write this I am still in a state of half sleep. I have just had the worst dream of my life. **If indeed it was a dream.**

I think it started at the dismal abode of the Snoxells. I found myself in the dark stairwell, fumbling about, trying to locate the secret doorway Nat had once shown me.

Prior to this I had presumably been envisaging bright sunshine, ergo lengthening the normal eye process of switching from canes to rods. Eventually, in that poor luminosity, I discerned sickly subfusc blue hues outlining the sought-after stone entrance. I shifted the slab and entered.

As I sidled down the first few steps, I became aware of a voice counting down my progress. Each step engendered a growing sense of foreboding and the disembodied voice encouraged this, in a hideous parody of the hypnotic technique used by me so often on my patients.

It suddenly became clear to me that my subconscious was telling me something about my life: that for some time I had not been following the Buddhist middle path. On the wheel of becoming, I had veered too far from the demoniac and too close to the angelic, and so my recompense was due. At this point the dream was lucid. I could have ended it there and then or gone off at a more pleasing tangent. If I had done this, I felt, my commitment to Zen would be revealed as mere sham. I had to go on; to lay myself open to the subcurrent.

I reached the penultimate step, trembling and covered in cold sweat. The horrid voice urged me on, suggesting that the final step would leave me in a completely terrified condition. Inexorably, I continued on my downward trajectory. My feet sank into terra incognita and for a moment I experienced **total panic**, then all-encompassing darkness.

A scene slowly unfurled before my hapless eyes, which were once again required to adjust to a new level of light, dusky by normal standards, but blinding after my brief plunge into the abyss. I was not in the cellar, but I was underground, in a kind of flooded catacomb. The water was yellow and malodorous; I struggled violently to avoid imbibing the malignant liquid. I soon found it was best not to move at all, for I then remained buoyant. The motionless subterranean river, despite its stagnant appearance, must, I thought, have certain properties in common with the Dead Sea. I was glad, in a perverse way, that relaxation was possible.

My musings were quickly curtailed, for obnoxious creatures loomed on the horizon. From very numerous tributaries all manner of corpses and decomposed bodies assailed my already incredulous and overworked eyes. The endless trail of long since deceased effluent, discharged from so many charnel houses, had succeeded in finding a means of propulsion where I had failed. I was soon caught up in the zombie flow. The movements were unbearable enough as it was, yet worse still I even **recognised several bone heads**, those where a few fleshly features still hung, but I could not name them. Still, as I gazed upon each semirecollected rotted countenance, each returned the glance with a revolting nod.

Some of the sickly sewage must have seeped into my eyes, for the dream was temporarily lost to me. Soon I became aware of my body once more. I was tumbling through what I can only describe as a **vivid void**, for it was light and delicate, but in essence just as foul as its superficial but ultimately false antithesis, the black abyss which I experienced at the bottom of the cellar staircase.

Emerging from the vivid void, I found myself watching the zombie-flow wend its way along a rickety road. Screaming skulls passed me, driven onward by their own foul and noisy breath. Skeletons of murderers ran into a red brick house which was dwarfed by its own cyclopean chimney stack belching out black bones and murky skulls. I watched as every corpse was cremated. Then the picture faded and was replaced by another.

In a grotto, Pan began to prescind his penis. I turned away, but the Greek god leapt upon me, thrusting the huge severed member down my throat. I have never before felt such a powerful combination of illness and exhilaration; the detached organ swiftly completed its passage through my body and was borne aloft into the skies, through a hole in the cave roof, by cracked, withered and quivering aeon-aged angels to some unknown destination, or **patron**. The self-amputee had disappeared too.

I was just preparing myself for the dissolution of this episode, when I was, once more, taken aback. I found the grotto metamorphosing in a subtle, virtually imperceptible manner all around me: black arcadia and crumbling vistas, until finally the image halted, when it reached a type of warped arboretum which made even the most grotesque bonsai look quite wholesome. The twigs and branches grew downwards, and thrust themselves so deeply into the satanic-looking soil that they rapidly became indistinguishable from the mad, twisted roots. Even the wildest works of Rodolphe Bresdin fail to hint at such morbid growths as these. This tree garden became so thoroughly dense that all light was blotted out.

By and by, scintillating sparks impinged upon my dream-consciousness. I feared forest fire, and attempted to negotiate a path through the bountiful profusions of perennial plants, but could find none. They too had proved purely transient, or perhaps they had merely continued on their downward spiral, burrowing into the ground. This fancy was unfounded too for the soil was undisturbed and even felt smooth underfoot.

The spangles overhead, I decided, were stars. There were too many of course, as if they had multiplied in order to lessen and eventually eradicate the intolerably awesome spaces that gape betwixt them. I had hoped to witness this but it was not to be, for stars are like cats, solitary and jealous, and the sun came up, driving its siblings away.

Previously, enclosed areas and monsters had oppressed me. Now I beheld a wide deserted market place, which I found equally relentless. Nor was I relieved to find, each time I blinked, the scene changing in some devastating manner. A road stretched straight into the distance, mocking its circumbendibus crematorium-serving predecessor, with tumbling columns running along its length. Atop each toppling tower was something horrendous; precisely what, I shall never know, for my eyelids descended, changing the outlook to a reconstruction of my student days: discussions in the early hours, focusing, on this occasion, on cloud formations: can they ever take on a recognisably human form? I heard no debate, for shut-eye curtailed this recollection.

I had to have rest, so I hid my face in my hands. It all became internal. I lost my way in the labyrinth of nightmare, time, vision, memory. A wizened wizard appeared on a vast plain, culled from the real world which I have inhabited—for these past forty odd years?

The wizened wizard manipulated clouds, painting with them, making fearful forms which glowered and leered at me, something more than mere condensed watery vapour. I sought asylum, but the level tract of ground on which the wizened wizard and I stood was unblemished and met the blue sky on all horizons. The wizard toyed with his cloud puppets, not only overhead but also in the distance, for great monsters lumbered at the periphery where earth met sky.

Other personages began to assemble before my eyes. It was like watching so many postmortems, speeded-up and in reverse. The ground sprouted pigments, trapped within vilely shaped miniscule shards—the work of an army of mad mosaicists, perchance—which, all of a sudden, were lit up in certain areas from underneath, sending up shafts of horridly hued light, an evil addition to the wizard's already formidable putrid paintbox and one which he made full use of, creating colour clouds of noxious intensity.

Crowds welled up from nowhere, looking most at home in the dreamscape—or whatever it was—leaving me as the only incongruity, with mounting trepidation. But such phrases cannot begin to convey how I felt. I never thought that I would find myself relating to Nat's "doom-laden" feelings, but even his ultra-way-out artworks, with all the benefit of having studied the masters of the macabre and fantastic (Bosch, Goya, Fuseli, Dore and that weird art brut phenomenon that so obsessed him), could not begin to prepare one for this assault; how could it? Creativity, however pessimistic it appears, is quintessentially optimistic, proven by the fact of its actual existence.

Relaxation and meditation were closed worlds to me, ergo I chose to occupy my intellect with as many ideas as possible, but even this last bastion of my sensibilities began to crumble as I was plagued by simonists, rattling obnoxious relics in my face. They eventually trampled me underfoot, leaving in their wake a smell that only accumulated centuries can yield. Their place was taken by oneirologists squabbling with oneiromanists. I had expected even greater tortures. The palaver would have been quite comic, were it not for the fact that not even black humour can exist at such times.

This fracas was in turn succeeded by an ensemble clustered about a little black box shedding blue hues, though with all the strange colours bursting out so abundantly, individual local colour was difficult to discern.

A full-length mirror was brought before me. The reflection was my own much-dishevelled self, only something aside from my decayed state was disturbing: it was not a false reflection I gazed upon. It was a perfect image—with nothing reversed. Childhood reading had led me to expect that I might walk into this peculiar looking glass, and I made towards it, but it was my other self that emerged first, stepping into my domain. We indulged in a mutual stare: the eye that saw itself. We meshed and merged together, my Siamese twin and I, and strode on, feeling hideously whole.

I gazed into the fiendish firmament, to sample the wizened wizard's latest manifestations. The sky was puce, like the fleece of a massive flea. I gained a glimpse of every dream that was being dreamed by humans, creatures and things at that one moment. "Mind expansion: brain used to full capacity for the first time", rumbled a voice in my head. The sky lapsed, to an almost restful orange glow. I was able to walk quite freely.

The flow of images triggered reactions and profound implications. Each sight was somehow already known to me: my worst fears confirmed.

A hundred-year-old sermon was delivered. This was the speaker's age, the speech having begun at birth. She stood on a plinth which bore the inscription: "You discovered the facts of my life and crucified me upon them". She was the **motherman**. "Are you the poison-person?" she seemed to be saying, although it could have been anything for there were many menagerie-esque squallings going on besides.

Out of the corner of my eye, I saw the founder of Zen, with withered legs. He scuttled along on strengthened arms, rather like the "half boy" in Tod Browning's film *Freaks*.

Egged on, I began to run. I soon found this to be an egregious blunder, as I stumbled painfully over bound bodies, babies bound to blueness in swaddling. Screaming, mummified babies. A wicked winding sheet covered them in a more permanent death. I rolled away from the mass murder as nightmares appeared up in the sky. A spindly giant tore them down and gobbled them up, like Saturn devouring his children. I rose and travelled a road of infant corpses. I finally felt myself to be at the perverse penetralia of this mad maze.

For his piece-de-resistance, the wizard had created an atmosphere of unequalled horror, primarily subfusc and nigrescent. Sinister pinnacles surrounded a loathsome assemblage, gathered in stygian celebration. Various drones, all at different pitches, polluted the air from various directions, making even musica in diabola seem mundane. Indeed, the ensuing echoing and awesome acoustics were the very enemy of music incarnate.

A grotesque with a hollowed out head and titanic green fungus sprouting vigorously, visibly growing where brains should have been, was shuffling among us. Creatures of predatory inclinations snapped at the morbid growths; indeed, all and sundry soon partook of the pickings. I too ate one of the tarnished toadstools. Almost in sympathy with the host supplier of fodder, weightlessness was induced in the skulls of black robed beings with conoid heads, and their brains flew out. Creatures of higher echelons were unaffected, and I was counted amongst their number. The unfortunates then circled us, running in a wild pack, like decapitated chickens.

The climax was approaching, I was convinced of that. The ground crumbled and quaked, emitting sounds that were even more frightful than that foul antimusic. A black idol shot out of an aperture and was soon towering above us. It was bedecked in ecclesiastical costume; atop its head was a manic mitre which seemed to have a life all its own. Around its neck was a necklace of weird skulls, of which unicorn and horned human were the least obscure. It had spinning, globular eyes. Lamely, I made up my mind to leave this place. Succumbing to weaknesses is, after all, just as Zen as overcoming them, providing one realises what one is doing. However, I just couldn't bestir myself.

And then the vomiting started. Very numerous were the disgorgings, but spewing what? I could not tell, despite being covered with the stuff.

Then the **voice**: an amalgamation of all earthly languages, ancient and modern. All idioms and dialects issued forth from the black idol. Even the worst excesses of science fiction could not even have guessed at such a sound.

I awoke cleaner and feeling more refreshed than ever before. The cathartic nightmare had been almost worthwhile.

I went into my study, to check the allusions and references made in my dreams. My hand idly strayed to a book that was not mine: it was the borrowed tome to which Nat had once been drawn.

I made a sudden intuitive connection: **I was still dreaming**.

The floorboards beneath my feet splintered and shattered. A rock shot up, with a ferocity equal to that which the black idol had used. My word processor, printer and other possessions were crushed, but I was unharmed and quite able to peruse the phenomenon. The rock stopped just short of the ceiling; it cracked open, revealing a **gigantic fossilised foetus**. It had been so perfectly preserved in the stone that it was still pink in colour and quite free from any bad smell.

The ancient offspring **screamed**.

Rapid, intense visions overlapping; deep, interlocking simulacrum; sinister concatenation that should never be made: these and the like, coupled with cessation of bodily functions, led me to believe that I was dead.

To my chagrin this was not the case. Even now I remain in a trance, with **that scream** still ringing in my ears.

Dreams **are** important. Far more important than the drab consciousness of our awakened state.

I have reason to believe that it is possible to enter the dreamworld entirely.

* * *

173

Dr. Rodney H. Dweller became a professional violinist for a short time, playing on an ad hoc basis for numerous London ensembles, before retiring to a Tibetan Monastery in Scotland, where he refused to see any friends and where, much against the abbot's advice, he took a vow of silence. He insisted on being locked into a one-man cell. His mother arranged for special food to be sent to him as well as a copious supply of pens, pencils and paper. He ignored the former, but greatly utilised the latter.

Rodney H. Dweller disappeared on the 30 April 1986. His cell was crammed with manuscripts penned entirely by himself whilst under self-hypnosis. Many of these works are still being translated today, largely from the Tibetan. A forbidden Latin version of the Necronomicon *was destroyed on sight by the enlightened monks.*

Dweller's diaries were also found in the cell, but most of the entries had been obliterated. This book contains the remainder, which are of a personal nature. Those wishing for a more scientific study are advised to consult the medical journals of the time, which published numerous articles by Dr. Dweller about the case of the primal screamer.

Entries after the 21 November 1985 were made in a script and language which have yet to be identified.

The Story of Crass
George Berger
978-1-60486-037-5
$20.00

Crass was the anarcho-punk face of a revolutionary movement founded by radical thinkers and artists Penny Rimbaud, Gee Vaucher and Steve Ignorant. When punk ruled the waves, Crass waived the rules and took it further, putting out their own records, films and magazines and setting up a series of situationist pranks that were dutifully covered by the world's press. Not just another iconoclastic band, Crass was a musical, social and political phenomenon.

Commune dwellers who were rarely photographed and remained contemptuous of conventional pop stardom; their members explored and finally exhausted the possibilities of punk-led anarchy. They have at last collaborated on telling the whole Crass story, giving access to many never-before seen photos and interviews.

Reviews:

"Lucid in recounting their dealings with freaks, coppers, and punks the band's voices predominate, and that's for the best." —*The Guardian UK*

"Thoroughly researched...chockful of fascinating revelations...it is, surprisingly, the first real history of the pioneers of anarcho-punk." —*Classic Rock*

"They (Crass) sowed the ground for the return of serious anarchism in the early eighties." —Jon Savage, *England's Dreaming*

About the Author:

George Berger has written for *Sounds*, *Melody Maker*, and Amnesty International amongst others. His previous book was a biography of the Levellers: *State Education/No University.*

Spray Paint the Walls:
The Story of Black Flag
Stevie Chick
978-1-60486-418-2
$19.95

Black Flag were the pioneers of American Hardcore, and this is their blood-spattered story. Formed in Hermosa Beach, California in 1978, for eight brutal years they made and played brilliant, ugly, no-holds-barred music on a self-appointed touring circuit of America's clubs, squats and community halls. They fought with everybody: the police, the record industry and even their own fans. They toured overseas on pennies a day and did it in beat-up trucks and vans.

Spray Paint The Walls tells Black Flag's story from the inside, drawing on exclusive interviews with the group's members, their contemporaries, and the bands they inspired. It's the story of Henry Rollins, and his journey from fan to iconic frontman. And it's the story of Greg Ginn, who turned his electronics company into one of the world's most influential independent record labels while leading Black Flag from punk's three-chord frenzy into heavy metal and free-jazz. Featuring over 30 photos of the band from Glen E. Friedman, Edward Colver, and others.

Praise:
"Neither Greg Ginn nor Henry Rollins sat for interviews but their voices are included from earlier interviews, and more importantly Chuck Dukowski spoke to Chick—a first I believe. The story, laid out from the band's earliest practices in 1976 to its end ten years later, makes a far more dramatic book than the usual shelf-fillers with their stretch to make the empty stories of various chart-toppers sound exciting and crucial and against the odds." —Joe Carducci, formerly of SST Records

About the Author:
Stevie Chick has been writing about music for more than ten years, contributing to such titles as *MOJO, The Guardian, Kerrang!, NME, Melody Maker,* and *Careless Talk Costs Lives* and editing underground rock magazine *Loose Lips Sink Ships* with photographer Steve Gullick. He is the author of *Psychic Confusion: The Sonic Youth Story.* He lives in South London.

Lonely Hearts Killer
Tomoyuki Hoshino
Translated by
Adrienne Carey Hurley
978-1-60486-084-9
$15.95

What happens when a popular and young emperor suddenly dies, and the only person available to succeed him is his sister? How can people in an island country survive as climate change and martial law are eroding more and more opportunities for local sustainability and mutual aid? And what can be done to challenge the rise of a new authoritarian political leadership at a time when the general public is obsessed with fears related to personal and national "security"? These and other provocative questions provide the backdrop for this powerhouse novel about young adults embroiled in what appear to be more private matters – friendships, sex, a love suicide, and struggles to cope with grief and work.

PM Press is proud to bring you this first English translation of a full-length novel by the award-winning author Tomoyuki Hoshino.

Praise:

"A major novel by Tomoyuki Hoshino, one of the most compelling and challenging writers in Japan today, *Lonely Hearts Killer* deftly weaves a path between geopolitical events and individual experience, forcing a personal confrontation with the political brutality of the postmodern era. Adrienne Hurley's brilliant translation captures the nuance and wit of Hoshino's exploration of depths that rise to the surface in the violent acts of contemporary youth." —Thomas LaMarre, William Dawson Professor of East Asian Studies, McGill University

About the Author:

Since his literary debut in 1997, Tomoyuki Hoshino has published twelve books on subjects ranging from 'terrorism' to queer/trans community formations; from the exploitation of migrant workers to journalistic ethics; and from the Japanese emperor system to neoliberalism. He is also well known in Japan for his nonfiction essays on politics, society, the arts, and sports, particularly soccer. He maintains a website and blog at http://www.hoshinot.jp/.

A Mix of Bricks & Valentines
G. W. Sok
Introduction by John Robb
978-1-60486-499-1
$20.00

G.W. Sok co-founded of the internationally acclaimed independent Dutch music group The Ex in 1979. He became the singer and lyricist, more or less by coincidence, since he wrote the occasional poem and nobody else wanted to sing. At the same time he turned himself into a graphic designer of record sleeves, posters, and books. Together with The Ex he was awarded the Dutch Pop Prize of 1991. The band is well known for its energetic live performances, their inventive music, and for their politically outspoken and thought-provoking lyrics. After 1,400 concerts in Holland and abroad, and 25 record albums later, G.W. Sok decided to leave the group at the end of 2008.

A Mix of Bricks & Valentines showcases the lyrics G.W. Sok wrote during his three decade period of Ex-istance. More than 250 songs of agitprop lyrics, poetry, and rantings are included along with an introduction by the author discussing his development as a writer. A foreword by English journalist, author, and musician John Robb (the Membranes, *Punk: An Oral History*, and *Death to Trad Rock*) puts the work of G.W. Sok into perspective.

A Mix of Bricks & Valentines is written with a sharp pen; provocative, creative, and witty, everything punk and art intended to be from the start. And yes, it can be quite loud at times, too

About the Author:
G.W. Sok is a co-founder of the music-group The Ex, and was their vocalist/lyricist from 1979–2009. Together they played almost 1,400 concerts and released 25 albums. Currently he is a graphic designer, actor, and musician, playing with the Amsterdam-based guitar-duo Two Pin Din and with the French trio Cannibales & Vahinés.

PM Press was founded at the end of 2007 by a small collection of folks with decades of publishing, media, and organizing experience. PM Press co-conspirators have published and distributed hundreds of books, pamphlets, CDs, and DVDs. Members of PM have founded enduring book fairs, spearheaded victorious tenant organizing campaigns, and worked closely with bookstores, academic conferences, and even rock bands to deliver political and challenging ideas to all walks of life. We're old enough to know what we're doing and young enough to know what's at stake.

We seek to create radical and stimulating fiction and non-fiction books, pamphlets, t-shirts, visual and audio materials to entertain, educate and inspire you. We aim to distribute these through every available channel with every available technology—whether that means you are seeing anarchist classics at our bookfair stalls; reading our latest vegan cookbook at the café; downloading geeky fiction e-books; or digging new music and timely videos from our website.

PM Press is always on the lookout for talented and skilled volunteers, artists, activists and writers to work with. If you have a great idea for a project or can contribute in some way, please get in touch.

Friends of PM allows you to directly help impact, amplify, and revitalize the discourse and actions of radical writers, filmmakers, and artists. It provides us with a stable foundation from which we can build upon our early successes and provides a much-needed subsidy for the materials that can't necessarily pay their own way. You can help make that happen – and receive every new title automatically delivered to your door once a month – by joining as a Friend of PM Press. And, we'll throw in a free T-Shirt when you sign up.
Just go to www.pmpress.org to sign up. Your Visa or Mastercard will be billed once a month, until you tell us to stop. Or until our efforts succeed in bringing the revolution around. Or the financial meltdown of Capital makes plastic redundant. Whichever comes first.

PM Press
PO Box 23912
Oakland CA 94623
510-658-3906
www.pmpress.org